Handle with Care

KYSA STEELE

To everyone who's dealt with or is currently dealing with a chronically ill pet, or those who are chronically ill themselves.

Keep fighting and remember the good days.

Contents

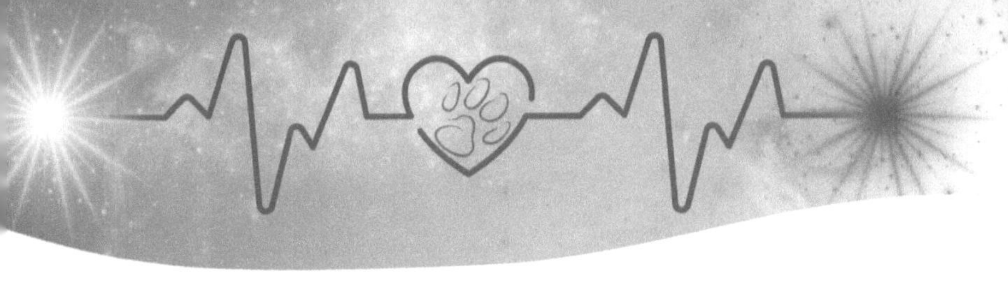

Foreword

This story is not written in my usual humorous style. It was a very difficult story to write, as it is based on my own journey with a chronically ill kitty.

If you're not in a place for this kind of story right now, please take care of yourself.

No, the cat does not die—but there's no magical cure either. Just good days and bad days. If you are okay with that, please read on.

This is Missi's story.

ONE

The Chair

MISSI

The sun finds me first.

Of course it does. The window faces east, the chair sits where the light pools, and here I am. The fabric holds my shape—a shallow bowl worn into the cushion from a hundred naps, a thousand afternoons, all the slow hours spent soaking in warmth while dust drifted through the light.

I stretch. Back legs first, driving against the armrest until claws snag the weave. Then the front. Spine arching. A long pull of muscle and fur. *I am awake. The day can begin.*

The kitchen smells like static and burned toast. The Witch is standing at the counter, back to me, but I know what she's doing. I can hear the *tink-tink-tink* of the metal spoon against ceramic. She isn't holding it. She never does before her first cup.

I trot in, tail held high. The air in here feels thick—like the sky right before a storm breaks. It makes my whiskers twitch.

"Morning, Missi," she says. She doesn't turn around. She doesn't have to.

The kettle on the stove screams, then cuts off abruptly as she flicks a finger. The water lifts itself—a shimmering, steaming ribbon—and pours perfectly into the mug. No splashes. I weave between her ankles. *Enough with the floating water. The bowls. Look at the bowls.* They are empty. A tragedy. An oversight of criminal proportions.

"Alright, alright," she sighs.

She reaches for the cabinet—not the handle, just the air in front of it. The wood groans, the latch clicks, and the heavy bag of kibble slides out, drifting down to the counter with the grace of a falling feather. I respect the efficiency, mostly. It gets the food into the bowl faster. She snaps her fingers. The bag splits. The kibble rains down—*clatter-clatter-clatter*—filling the ceramic dishes.

Only then does she pick up her mug. The spoon stops spinning and drops onto the counter with a wet clatter. The static fades. The air goes back to smelling like regular morning dust and coffee. Magic is useful, I suppose. But it doesn't taste like anything.

Jake is finishing breakfast in his spot behind the water bowl, where he thinks he's invisible. I don't need to look. I know the sound of his chewing—quick, nervous bites, glances flicking to the door, to the shadow in the corner that has never been anything but a shadow.

Jake is afraid of everything. Loud noises. Unfamiliar smells. His own reflection, if the light catches wrong. An orange giant terrified of the world. I was the scared one when we were kittens—he was the brave one. Somewhere along the way, we traded.

The Witch is at the table now. Papers spread out—white squares that smell like dust and old ink, covered in the little scratches that mean something to her and nothing to me. She's got that unwashed morning scent, herbs and sleep and the soap she uses. Her hair keeps falling into her face.

She doesn't see me coming. Mistake.

I cross the room. Jump. One clean motion, landing between her and the papers. They're smooth under my paws, slippery.

"Missi—"

I sit on the page she was looking at. The paper crinkles, warm from the sun. Mine now.

"I was reading that."

I look at her. She knows what I want. Why do they always need it explained? I head-butt her hand. *Pet. Me.*

She laughs—a wonderful sound, soft, no sharp edges. Her hand finds the spot behind my left ear, the one that makes my eyes droop. She smells of coffee and the herbs drying in the window. She knows the pressure. She knows the rhythm.

"Demanding little thing," she murmurs.

I purr. It starts deep in the chest, vibrating against my ribs. This is the morning. The sun, the scratch of nails through fur. I lean into her hand. Harder. She obliges. Her other hand joins the first, working down my spine. The restlessness I carry—always scanning, always ready—goes quiet. It only does this for her.

"You're going to smear the ink."

Let it smear.

She sighs, but she's smiling. Her thumb traces the edge of my ear. *Yes. There.* We stay like that—her hands, my purr, the morning stretching out lazy and warm. Nowhere else to be.

Then, the shift. Like the sun slipping behind a cloud. The touch, perfect a second ago, becomes too much. Overstimulating. Static. I duck away, drop from the table, shake my fur back into place.

"You're welcome," she says to my retreating back.

I flick my tail. She knows I'm grateful. I don't need to say it.

The sunny spot by the window is mine, too.

The heat sinks through my fur, into muscle, into bone. I tuck my paws beneath me and let it pool there. Grooming time. Face first—paw dampened, drawn across whiskers, cheek, eyes. Ears. Chest. My tail comes last.

I pull it close, working through the fur with my teeth. Smoothing. Straightening. Then my tongue finds the place where the fur grows wrong. A ridge. Skin tight and shiny.

The scar.

I don't remember the pain anymore. I was too small. I remember the cold—deep, bone-aching cold that made me stupid and slow. A dark, cramped space smelling of metal and old oil. Then the rumble, vibration shaking through the ground, up through my ribs. Then the heat. A flash of it. Searing. Running without knowing where, yowling without knowing why. *Out. Just out.*

Only Jake and I made it.

I don't think about the others. It's been too long. The cold belongs to a different cat. I have the chair. I have the sunny spot. I have Jake, who was there in the dark, who nudged me when I froze. I remember his heat against my flank—a small furnace when everything else was cold. Now he flinches at brooms. Maybe he used it all up that night. Spent his whole allowance of courage on the one moment that mattered. At least, that's how I understand it.

The scar is smooth under my tongue. Just a part of the geography now. I finish grooming it and move on. That was before. This is home.

I'm halfway through my shoulder when the closet door opens.

It's a specific squeak. A high, rusted hinge sound that means only one thing. Jake hears it from three rooms away. I feel the vibration of his panic through the floorboards before I even see him. He comes skidding around the corner, claws scrabbling uselessly on the hardwood, taking the turn too wide and crashing shoulder-first into the wall. He recovers, eyes huge, pupils swallowed by black terror, and scrambles under the sofa. Deep under. Far enough back that only the tip of his orange tail betrays him.

The Witch steps out. In her hand, The Enemy.

It is a stick. With straw tied to the end.

"Sorry, guys," she says. "It's a disaster in here."

She sweeps. *Swish, scuff. Swish, scuff.* It is the most boring sound in the world. But to Jake, it is the jaws of death. I hear him whimpering from under the sofa—a low, pathetic keening. The bristles push a pile of dust and shed fur toward me.

I do not move.

The Witch stops. She looks at me. I look at her. I am washing my paws. I am busy.

"Move, Missi."

I stop washing. I stare at the broom. I dare it to come closer. *Touch me with that straw and see what happens.*

She sighs. "Fine. Be an obstacle."

She sweeps around me. Careful strokes, giving me a wide berth. As it should be. Under the sofa, Jake trembles in his own dust bunny. I flick an ear in his direction. *Embarrassing.* But he came when I called, once. That has to count for something.

TWO

Ordinary

WITCH

She wakes before the sun does. Not by choice. By decree.

The decree takes the form of twelve pounds of tortoiseshell sitting on her diaphragm, staring down at her with the intensity of a creature who has been starving for exactly four hours. Missi's eyes catch the faint pre-dawn light from the window, two gleaming coins of judgment.

"I'm awake," she croaks. "I'm—ow."

A single claw. Just a reminder.

"Okay. Getting up."

Missi launches herself off the bed—a solid *thump* against the floorboards—and trots toward the door, tail high like a flag. *Follow. Now.*

The Witch rolls out of the warmth. The cottage floor is freezing—the kind of cold that seeps up through the soles of your feet and settles in the ankles. She shuffles to the kitchen, the air smelling of stale woodsmoke and the sharp, coppery tang of the spell she worked last night to keep the drafts out. It obviously didn't work.

Jake is already there, wedged into the safe corner between the cabinet and the wall. He flinches when she enters, ears going flat, then settles when he realizes it's just her. His whole body relaxes in stages—ears first, then shoulders, then the tight curl of his tail.

"Morning, big guy."

She leans against the counter, too tired to find the scoop. The kibble spell is small, habitual—the kind of magic that costs almost nothing after years of repetition. She flicks a finger. The cabinet latch clicks. The bag slides out, floating heavily through the air. A quick twitch of her wrist, and the kibble rains into the bowls—*clatter-clatter-clatter*.

Missi doesn't care about the magic; she only cares about the physics of food hitting ceramic. She dives in, eating as if she's been deprived for weeks rather than hours. Jake waits, checking the shadows, checking the doorway, checking the space behind him, before taking his first nervous bite. Two cats. Same litter. One thinks she's a queen; the other thinks he's prey.

She watches them eat. Missi, aggressive and certain. Jake, hunched and wary, glancing up between every few bites. They came from the same cold, dark place—she knows this, though she doesn't know the details. Whatever happened to them before, it left opposite marks.

The kettle sits cold on the stove. She could heat it with a thought—it would be faster—but she's saving her energy. The rent is due in four days, and real spell-work takes calories she can't always afford to replace. She reaches for the matches instead. Ordinary fire is cheaper.

The match flares, sulfur-sharp, and she holds it to the kindling until the flame catches. While the water heats, she stands at the window and watches the sky lighten. Gray bleeding into pale pink. Another day.

The general store smells of sawdust and pickled beets.

It's inventory day. Bessa, the owner, is buried behind a tower of invoices at the back counter, her spectacles perched on the end of her nose, her pen scratching furiously. That leaves the Witch to wrestle the crates of winter stock that arrived yesterday and are currently blocking the entire back hallway.

It's not glamorous work. It's lifting, counting, and recording. Her shoulders ache by the second crate. Her lower back joins the complaint by the fourth. But she's good with numbers—always has been. She likes the way they line up, the way a column of figures balances out if you just stare at it long enough. In a life that often feels like it's fraying at the edges, a balanced ledger is a small, quiet mercy.

"You're dragging today," Bessa calls out from her fortress of paperwork.

"Cats," the Witch says, hefting a crate of candles onto the shelf. "Missi decided dawn was merely a suggestion."

Bessa snorts. "Familiars. Little tyrants, all of them." She pauses, finally looking over her spectacles. "How is the other one? The orange?"

"Jake?" The Witch wipes dust from her hands onto her apron. "He's... Jake. Still afraid of the broom. Still afraid of the wind. But he eats. He sits with me at night."

"Brave isn't about not being scared," Bessa says, eyes returning to her own mountain of invoices. "Brave is doing it anyway. You remember that."

The Witch nods, turning back to the crates. She thinks about Jake creeping out from under the bed every evening, crossing the vast, terrifying expanse of the floor to settle near her feet. Scared of everything, but there anyway. Yeah. She knows something about that.

"Excuse me? Miss?"

The Witch looks up from the crate of candles. It's Mrs. Gable from down the lane—a small woman with worried eyes and hands that never stop moving. She's clutching a heavy woolen coat that looks like it's lost a fight with a moth colony.

"Bessa said you might... take a look?" Mrs. Gable asks hopefully. "I know it's not your trade, but—"

The Witch takes the coat, spreading it across the counter. The damage is worse than it looked at first glance. Three holes, edges fraying, the weave coming apart in a slow unraveling that will only get worse with time.

"The weave is gone, Mrs. Gable. I can't knit air."

"Just a binding? To keep it from unraveling further?" The woman's voice goes thin. "It's for my husband. The winter's coming on, and we can't afford—" She stops herself. Swallows. "We can't afford to replace it."

It's not in her job description. Bessa doesn't pay her for

this. She thinks of the kettle she didn't heat this morning, the energy she banked for real spell-work. But the coat is thin, and Mrs. Gable's hands are red from the cold, and the Witch knows exactly what it feels like to dread the coming frost with holes in your pockets.

"Put it flat on the counter."

She places her hands over the fabric and closes her eyes. She doesn't reach for the deep magic—the stuff that moves water or lights fires. She reaches for the small, tedious magic. The *stitching* magic. The kind that's all precision and patience and no flash at all. It feels like pulling a thread through her own teeth.

A sharp, thin headache spikes behind her left eye. She pushes the energy into the wool, fusing the fraying edges, locking the fibers together. It takes thirty seconds. It feels like thirty minutes. The world goes slightly gray at the edges, and she has to grip the counter to stay steady. When she pulls back, the holes are still there—she's not a miracle worker—but the edges are sealed tight. It won't get worse.

"Oh," Mrs. Gable breathes. "Oh, thank you." She digs into her purse and puts two silver coins on the counter. Her hands are shaking slightly. "I know it's not much—"

It's too much for a patch job. It's not enough for the headache.

"Keep it warm," the Witch says, pocketing the coins. Her own hands are trembling now. Low sugar. She needs lunch, and she needs to sit down, and she needs to stop giving pieces of herself away for less than they cost.

Mrs. Gable leaves, clutching the coat like a treasure. Bessa watches the whole transaction from her perch.

"You're too soft," she says. "You should charge double for structural work."

"It's just a coat, Bessa."

"It's your energy. You can't spend it twice."

The Witch nods. She knows. She touches the pocket of her apron, feeling the thin, reassuring weight of the week's wages, then her temple, where the headache still pulses. Steady. It's not much, but it's steady.

The apothecary is on the way home, tucked between the chandler's shop and a boarded-up storefront that used to sell charms. The Witch has been coming here for years— long enough that the bell over the door feels like a greeting, and the smell of dried herbs and tinctures feels like comfort.

The old man behind the counter knows her order before she reaches him.

"Flea prevention?" he asks, already reaching for the shelf. "And the joint supplement?"

"And the calming tincture." She lines the coins up on the counter. Silver, copper, copper. It leaves her purse feeling dangerously light.

"Storm coming?"

"Always is, for Jake."

The apothecary wraps the glass vials in brown paper, his movements practiced and efficient. "You take good care of them. Better than some take care of their kids."

"They're all I've got."

It sounds sad when she says it out loud, so she forces a smile. It's not sad. It's just true. Missi and Jake and the drafty cottage and the steady work at Bessa's—this is her life. It's small, but it's hers.

While the apothecary ties the bundle with string, the Witch wanders to the front display. There's a basket near the register filled with dried catnip mice. Not the cheap stuff that smells like sawdust, but the potent, velvet-leaf catnip imported from the coast. The kind that makes Jake forget he's afraid of his own shadow for an hour. The kind that makes Missi drool with undignified abandon, much to her later embarrassment.

She picks one up. It crinkles satisfyingly in her hand. The fabric is soft, well-made. It would last.

She checks the price tag. Four coppers. She runs the math. *Rent. Food. Tincture. Firewood.* If she buys the mouse, she skips the dried fruit for her own lunches next week. Or she waits another month to fix the draft in the bedroom window. Four coppers. It's nothing. It's everything.

She imagines Jake tossing it in the air, that rare unburdened look in his eyes. Missi rolling on her back, paws batting at nothing, dignity forgotten. The sound of them playing while she sits by the fire with her tea.

"Adding that to the pile?" the apothecary asks.

The Witch hesitates. Her thumb strokes the velvet fabric.

"No," she says. Her voice is steady, practiced. "Not today."

She puts the mouse back in the basket. It sits on top of the pile, cheerful and unreachable.

The walk home takes her through the market square, past the well, past the row of cottages with their neat gardens and their smoke-curling chimneys. The light is going gold and soft, the day tilting toward evening. Her feet know the route without her thinking about it.

The cottage comes into view—small, stone-walled, the thatch needing repair she can't afford. But the windows are glowing with the banked fire she left this morning, and even from here she can see a shadow moving behind the glass. Missi, probably. Watching for her.

She's barely through the door when Missi hits her ankle.

It's not a greeting—it's a collision. Twelve pounds of tortoiseshell ramming into her leg with enough force to make her stumble. Missi looks up, tail lashing, eyes bright with accusation. *Finally. You have returned from the hunting grounds. Where is the tribute?*

"Hello to you too," she sighs, dropping her bag by the door.

She scoops the cat up—dense, warm, immediately boneless against her chest. The purring starts before she even finds the right spot under Missi's chin, a deep rattle that vibrates through her ribs. This. This is the payoff. The aching shoulders from the crates, the headache from the coat, the thin purse and the cold floor—it buys this. This small, demanding creature who chose her and keeps choosing her, every single day.

Jake is in the window, watching. He doesn't come to greet her—too far, too open, too many steps across exposed floor. But he blinks. A slow, deliberate squeeze of his eyes. *Welcome home. I'm glad you're back. I'm staying here where it's safe, but I'm glad.*

She smiles at him. "Hey, buddy. I see you."

Dinner is toast and soup, eaten over the spread of bills on the table.

The wind has picked up, rattling the loose pane in the west window. Another three coppers she doesn't have. The roof groans overhead, and she tries not to think about what that sound means. She rubs her temples. The numbers on the page are starting to blur.

Rent. Heat. Food. Tincture.

It works. If she doesn't buy the new cloak she needs. If the winter isn't too harsh. If nothing breaks.

If nothing breaks.

A soft *thump* interrupts the math. Missi has jumped onto the table. She walks across the ledger, caring nothing for the carefully balanced columns, and sits directly on the total.

"I need that," the Witch says.

Missi stares at her. *No. You need this.*

From the rug by the fire, Jake lets out a long, shuddering sigh and tucks his nose under his tail. The fire pops. The wind rattles the windows again.

The Witch looks at the ledger, obscured by fur. She looks

at the fire. She looks at the empty soup bowl, the cat who refuses to let her work. She closes the ink pot.

The numbers will be there tomorrow. The roof will hold for one more night. She pushes the chair back and stands up. Missi makes a trilling sound of approval and leaps down, leading the way to the armchair by the fire like she's escorting royalty to the throne.

The Witch sits. The fire crackles. Missi claims her lap; Jake guards her feet. The cottage smells of herbs and woodsmoke, and the wind outside sounds very far away.

It is small, this life. It is drafty and expensive and always one disaster away from falling apart.

But it is theirs.

She closes her eyes, burying her hands in Missi's fur, and lets the purring fill the silence. The ledger can wait. The window can wait. The world and all its problems can wait.

For now, she is rich.

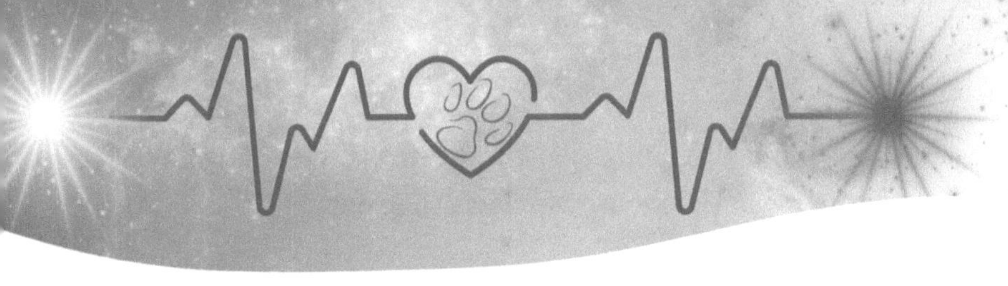

THREE

The Sore

MISSI

Something is wrong with my face.

I don't know when it started. Yesterday, maybe. The day before. A spot near my nose, right on the bridge where the fur is thinnest. It itches.

Not the pleasant, surface-level tickle of a stray hair. This is deep. It feels buried under the skin, wedged tight against the bone. A mosquito bite you can't reach. A vibration that won't stop.

I am in the sunny spot. Morning routine. I rub my face against the rough fabric of the armrest. *Hard.* I push my nose into the weave, grinding the spot against the friction. *Scritch. Scritch.*

For a second, the pressure drowns out the itch. It feels ecstatic. A moment of silence in the noise.

Then I pull back, and the itch floods back in—louder, hotter, sharper.

I lift my paw. I shouldn't use claws on my face. I know

this. It is a kitten mistake. But the itch is screaming now. I bring my back foot up. My claws slide out.

Dig.

My claw catches the spot. It tears something. A tiny, wet pop. The itch vanishes, replaced instantly by a bright, searing sting. *Better,* I think, shaking my head to clear the heat. *Pain is better than itching.*

I lick my paw. It tastes iron-sour. I try to move on. I groom my chest. The sting fades. The itch creeps back in, a slow tide rising under my fur.

I ignore it.

The Witch comes home smelling of sawdust and other people.

She smells of the shop—pickled beets and old receipts—and the crisp, cold air of the outside. I meet her at the door. I have been waiting. She has been gone. Compensation is required.

She scoops me up. This is correct. Her hands find the usual places—behind the ears, the hinge of the jaw. I settle against the wool of her coat. My eyes close. The world is right-side up.

Her thumb moves up the bridge of my nose. And passes over the spot.

I flinch.

It's involuntary. The skin is raw there now, tender from where I dug at it this morning.

"Hey," she says softly. "What was that?"

She shifts me, tilting my face toward the window light. Her eyes narrow. I don't like this. I am to be admired, not squinted at like one of her papers. Her finger touches the spot. It stings. I jerk my head away. My ears flatten. The sound that leaves my throat isn't a hiss—I don't hiss at her—but it's sharp. A hard exhale. *Don't.*

"Missi..." She's frowning. I hear the note in her voice. The worry note. "You've got something on your face. Dried food?"

She sets me down, but she doesn't let me go. She walks to the sink. Water runs. *No.* She comes back with a cloth. It smells of damp cotton and marigold water—earthy and bitter.

"Hold still," she says. "Let me just get it off."

I try to back up, but she has me cornered against the armchair. The cloth comes closer. It's cold. I turn my head.

"Missi, come on."

She pins me. Gently, but firmly. The hand that means *hold still whether you like it or not.* She presses the cool cloth against the bridge of my nose and *rubs.*

Fire.

It isn't dirt. It is a scab I made myself. And she just ripped it off. It feels like she scraped sandpaper over a burn.

I panic. I don't mean to, but the pain is sudden and bright. I scramble backward, claws scrabbling for purchase on the wool of the chair. I launch myself over the armrest, hitting the floor running.

"Missi!"

I don't stop. I run until I am under the dining table, in the deepest shadow I can find. My nose is throbbing now.

Truly throbbing. The Witch is standing by the chair. She is looking at the cloth in her hand.

I follow her gaze.

There is a small, bright speck on the white cotton. Pink. Blood.

She looks from the cloth to me. The worry note in her scent spikes into something sharper. Fear.

"It wasn't dirt," she whispers.

I stay under the table for a long time.

Eventually, the throbbing fades back to the hum of the itch. The Witch has gone back to her papers, though she keeps glancing at the floor. I need high ground.

I creep out and jump to the top of the bookshelf. This is my fortress. The highest point in the room. From here, I can see the garden through the top pane of the window. A blue jay lands on the fence. He is loud. Obnoxious. A screeching intruder in my kingdom.

Instinct takes over. I can still do this. I am still a hunter.

My jaw drops to make the sound—the *ek-ek-ek* of the hunter. The sound that says *I see you* and *I would eat you if there wasn't glass between us.* My mouth opens. The skin on my nose stretches.

The itch flares.

It pulls tight across the bridge of my nose. I snap my mouth shut. The sound dies in my throat.

The jay screams again, mocking. He hops along the fence, flicking his tail. I stare at him. I want to yell back. I want to tell him who owns this garden. But the sore is pulsing now, a hot wire pulled tight between my eyes. It hurts to chatter. It hurts to hunt.

I lower my head. I rub the side of my face against the sharp wooden corner of the bookshelf. Hard. Harder. *Scritch. Scritch.* It feels terrible. It feels amazing.

You win today, bird.

Jake appears at the bottom of the bookshelf.

He looks up. He moves the way he always moves—low, checking for monsters. But he is looking at me. He knows something is wrong. The air in the house has changed; it smells of iron and antiseptic and stress.

He stands on his hind legs, paws resting on the lower shelf, stretching his neck out, trying to sniff me. He is too far away. He drops back down and makes a small sound. A question. *Are we hiding?*

I don't answer him.

He jumps up. Not all the way—he's clumsy—but he scrambles onto the desk, then the chair, then the shelf. He is beside me now. He leans in. Whiskers brush my face. They hit the spot. It tickles. The tickle turns into an itch so violent I almost fall off the shelf.

I bat him away. Fast. *Pop.*

He flinches back, eyes wide and orange, nearly slipping off the edge. He regains his balance and sits just out of reach, watching me.

I'm fine, I want to tell him. *Go be afraid of the broom. Leave me alone.*

But he keeps watching. And the Witch keeps watching from the table. And the spot is still there, pulsing against my paw, hot and small and mine.

Night comes. I cannot settle.

I am in the chair. The cushion holds my shape. The fire is dying down. But I keep waking up. The spot won't let me forget. Every time I drift, my face presses against my paw, and the itch pulls me back. *I'm here,* it says. *Scratch me. Just once. Just a little.*

I rearrange myself. Looser. Tighter. Chin up. Chin down. Nothing works. The spot makes itself known, a dull heat in the dark that matches the beat of my heart.

Jake is asleep on the rug. Untroubled. The Witch is in her chair. She is not asleep. I can smell the worry on her—sharp, metallic, the way she smells when the money is low or the winter is coming. She isn't reading. She's just watching the fire.

I don't know what is wrong with me.

I have had injuries. Scars. Bites. Those made sense. Pain makes sense. You fight, you hurt, you heal. This has no sense. This is just... my own skin, betraying me.

I close my eyes. Try again.

The spot pulses in the dark. Patient. Waiting. I curl up tighter and pretend I can't feel it. But my claws are flexed. Waiting for me to sleep. Waiting for me to lose control so they can dig.

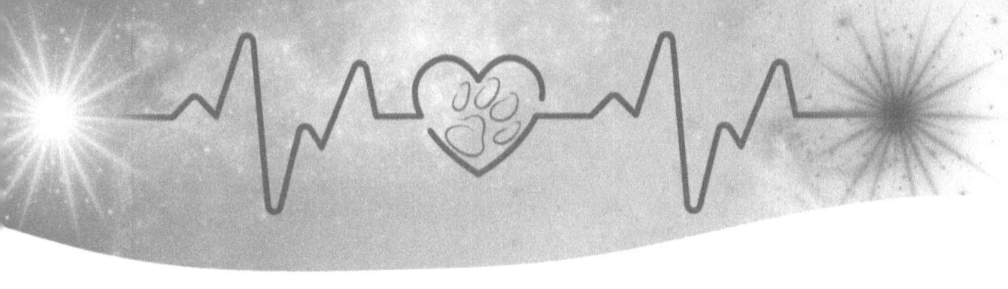

The First Visit

WITCH

The sore is worse.

I knew it before I even got out of bed—knew it from the way Missi was sleeping, curled too tight, face tucked into the darkest corner of the cushion. But I made myself check anyway. I knelt by the chair in the pale morning light and gently turned her head. Redder. The edges angrier than yesterday. The center is raw and weeping where she's been scratching it. It's not a scratch anymore. It's a crater.

It's probably nothing, I tell myself. Cats get things. Scrapes, acne, weird bumps. I don't believe me.

Missi blinks up, half-asleep. She makes a small questioning sound. *Why are you touching my face? It's too early.*

"I know," I murmur. "I'm sorry. Go back to sleep."

But I'm already doing the math. *Emergency fund: 12 silver. Rent: Due Tuesday. Healer consult: 5 silver.* The math is bad. The sore is worse. The carrier is in the closet. I haven't used it since the last check-up, months ago. When I pull it out, it smells like panic and old plastic—the ghost of every vet visit, every car ride, every betrayal. I set it on the floor. My hands are shaking slightly.

"No."

She doesn't say the word, but her body screams it. The moment the carrier appears, she's off the chair. Ears flat. Eyes wide with the particular betrayal of a cat who trusted you and has just discovered you are a jailer.

"Missi, please."

She bolts. What follows is undignified. A chase around the kitchen table. A near-miss under the bed. A standoff behind the bookshelf that ends with me flat on my stomach, arm extended into the dust bunnies, fingers brushing fur that retreats just out of reach.

"Please," I whisper to the darkness behind the books. "I know you hate this. But I'm scared."

Silence. A pair of green eyes gleaming in the shadows.

"I don't know what's happening to you," I admit. My voice cracks on the last word. I didn't mean for it to, but there it is. "And I need someone who does. I need help. I can't fix this by myself."

A long moment. Then, she emerges. Not willingly—her body is stiff with resentment—but she comes out. She allows herself to be picked up. She goes into the carrier with a yowl of protest that probably wakes the neighbors, and she does not stop complaining the entire walk to the village.

Jake watches from his spot behind the water bowl, eyes huge. He takes a hesitant step toward us, lets out a confused chirp. He doesn't understand. He just knows his sister is screaming and I am taking her away.

"It's okay," I tell him, though I'm not sure who I'm reassuring. "We'll be back soon. It's going to be okay." The words feel like lies in my mouth.

The Healer's office smells like bleach and sage.

There are other familiars in the waiting area. A toad in a glass case, pulsing wetly. A raven hunched in a covered cage, muttering words that sound like curses. A thin woman with a thin dog, both of them looking like they haven't slept in days. Missi has gone silent. This is worse than the screaming. Inside the carrier, she is a tight ball of fur pressed against the back corner, refusing to look at anything. *I am not here,* the silence says. *This is not happening. You are dead to me.*

"Missi?" An assistant appears at the door. "Come on back."

The exam room is cold metal and harsh light. I set the carrier on the table and open the door. Missi doesn't move.

"Come on, sweetie. It's okay."

It takes coaxing. It takes patience I don't have. Eventually, she stands on the metal table with the rigid posture of someone enduring a war crime. The Healer enters. Older woman, gray hair pinned back with iron clips.

She moves with the efficiency of someone who has seen a thousand sick animals and learned not to waste time on pleasantries.

"Face sore?"

"Yes. Appeared two days ago. Getting worse fast."

The Healer nods. She approaches calmly, giving Missi time to see her coming. Her hands find the edges of the sore, gentle but probing. Missi hisses. It's a small sound. But I've had Missi for six years. I have pulled thorns from her paws and bathed her when she fell in the rain barrel and held her through thunderstorms when Jake was too scared to come out from under the bed. She has never hissed at someone trying to help her.

I flinch. The sound cuts through all those years of trust like it was nothing.

The Healer steps back. Her expression goes neutral. Professional. "First, the light," she says.

She pulls a heavy, iron-cased wand from a drawer. She flicks a switch, and the room fills with a low, humming violet light. It makes my teeth look bright white. It makes the metal table look purple.

"Hold her steady."

I grip Missi's shoulders. She's trembling under my hands. The Healer passes the violet light over Missi's face. The sore looks black under the light. Crusted and dark.

"No glow," I whisper. I know enough about fungal infections to know that's good. "That means it's not Ringworm, right?"

The Healer sighs, clicking the light off. The room snaps back to harsh white normality. "Not necessarily. Only about half of Ringworm strains fluoresce. The lack of a glow doesn't clear her, unfortunately. It just means we don't get the easy answer today." She sets the wand down. "I still need to run a fungal culture. And a cytology. Until the culture proves otherwise, we have to treat it as positive."

"So a cream?"

"If it's Ringworm, yes," the Healer says. "But until we get the results back... you need to isolate her."

"Isolate?"

"Separate room. Door closed. No contact with the other cat. Limit your contact. Wash your hands with vinegar after you touch her."

I look at Missi. She is trembling, just slightly, her eyes fixed on the door like she's calculating escape routes. She hates closed doors. She hates being alone. And Jake—Jake falls apart if he can't see her.

"For how long?"

"The culture takes ten days to grow."

Ten days.

"And the house," the Healer adds. She's writing a prescription now, the quill scratching loudly in the quiet room. "Spores live on soft surfaces. Bedding. Rugs. Curtains." I think of my cottage. It is *entirely* soft surfaces. The armchair Missi sleeps in. The rug Jake drags himself across when he's feeling brave. The quilt on the bed that's been in my family for three generations.

"You need to wash everything," the Healer says, handing over the parchment. "Hot water. Bleach where you can. Vacuum the rest every day."

"Every day?"

"Spores are persistent. If you treat the cat but not the house, she'll just get reinfected."

I take the paper. It feels heavy. It's not just isolation. It's a war on my own home. I have to turn my sanctuary into a sterile zone, and I have to do it while working full time and keeping two cats apart and not knowing if any of it will even matter.

"Right," I say. "Vacuum. Bleach. Hot water." I put the list in my pocket next to the dwindling coins. I wonder how much bleach costs. I wonder how I'm going to explain to Bessa that I need to leave early every day to come home and clean.

"The culture will tell us more," the Healer says. Her voice softens, just slightly. "It might be nothing. Cats get things."

"And if it's not nothing?"

She meets my eyes. "Then we deal with it. One step at a time."

The walk home is longer than the walk there.

The carrier bangs against my leg with every step. Missi is silent inside it—not yowling anymore, just quiet in a way that feels like defeat. The streets of Miren Hollow are busy with afternoon traffic. People buying bread. People laughing outside the tavern. People whose cats aren't locked in plastic boxes, whose lives aren't about to be turned inside out for ten days or longer.

Ten days.

I try to make it manageable in my head. I'll move her litter box to the bedroom. I'll set up food and water in there.

I'll visit her as often as I can, wash my hands every time, keep the door closed between visits. And Jake— Jake will be alone. For the first time since they were kittens, he'll be alone. No sister to curl up with. No warm body to press against when the world gets too big and too scary.

It's just Ringworm, I tell myself. *It's annoying, but it's not life-threatening. We can do ten days.*

But the Healer's voice keeps replaying in my head. *It looks like Ringworm.* She didn't say *It is Ringworm.* She said *It looks like.* Which means it might be something else.

At home, I carry Missi straight to the bedroom.

Jake comes trotting out to greet us, chirping, tail high. Happy to see his sister return. He doesn't know what's coming. He just knows she was gone and now she's back, and everything should be normal again. I shut the door in his face.

I hear him stop on the other side. A confused silence. Then a scratch. *Let me in.*

"I can't, buddy," I whisper through the wood. "I'm sorry. I can't."

He scratches again. Harder. *Let me in. She's in there. I can smell her. Let me in.*

Inside the bedroom, I open the carrier. Missi shoots out like she's been launched. She runs to the door, expecting it to be the way back to her chair, her spot by the fire, her life. She finds the wood closed. She looks at me. *Open it.*

"I can't."

She yowls. It's a broken, confused sound—not anger, just bewilderment. She scratches at the frame. *Open it. Open it. Open it.* On the other side, Jake answers. His scratches match hers, a desperate duet through the door.

I sit down on the bed. My legs don't want to hold me up anymore.

This is for her own good. This is to keep Jake safe. This is just for ten days. I listen to Jake scratching on one side and Missi scratching on the other, and I try to believe that ten days is survivable.

I look at the bill the Healer gave me. Five silver for the visit. Three for the tests. Two for the antifungal cream, just in case. Ten silver. Almost the entire emergency fund, gone in one afternoon. I fold the paper and put it in my pocket. Rice and beans for the rest of the month. No dried fruit. No new cloak before winter.

From the bedroom, Missi cries again. From the living room, Jake answers.

I look at my hands. They held her. I touched the sore when I put her in the room. *Wash your hands,* the Healer said.

I go to the kitchen sink. I find the jug of vinegar under the counter—the cheap stuff I use for cleaning the windows. I pour it over my hands. It stings. I have a paper cut I didn't know about, and the acid finds it instantly. The smell hits me. Sharp. Sour. Aggressive. It smells like pickling jars and hard labor. It cuts through the smell of the herbs and the wood smoke and the faint lingering scent of cat fur. I scrub until my skin is red. I scrub until I can't smell the Healer's office anymore. I just smell the acid.

I dry my hands on a rough towel. They feel stripped. Clean, but the wrong kind of clean. Like I've scoured away something I needed.

Night comes, and I can't go to bed.

The bedroom is Missi's now. Her isolation ward. Her prison. I can't sleep in there—the Healer said to limit contact, and besides, the thought of lying in bed listening to her cry three feet away is more than I can take. I make up the couch instead. It's too short for me. My feet hang off the end, and the cushions sag in the middle, and the quilt I drag over myself smells like wood smoke and cat hair. Tomorrow I'll have to wash it. Tonight I just need something between me and the cold.

Jake finds me within minutes.

He creeps out from wherever he's been hiding—under the table, probably, or behind the bookshelf—and approaches the couch like it might be a trap. He sniffs the blanket. Sniffs my hand. Looks toward the closed bedroom door. *Where is she?*

"She's okay," I tell him. "She's just... she has to stay in there for a while. It's not forever."

He doesn't understand. Of course he doesn't. He just knows his sister is behind a door he can't open, making sounds he can't answer, and the world has stopped making sense. He jumps onto the couch. Curls up against my side, pressing close, trembling slightly. I put my hand on his back. His fur is soft and warm and I should probably wash my hands again after this, but I can't. I can't push him away too. He's already lost his sister tonight. I won't make him lose me.

"It's going to be okay," I whisper.

From the bedroom, Missi cries. Jake's ears flatten. He starts to rise, instinct telling him to hide—then stops. Presses closer instead. I feel his heart beating too fast against my ribs.

I stare at the ceiling. The fire has burned down to embers, and the room is getting cold, and somewhere in the dark Missi is alone and scared and I can't explain to her why.

Ten days.

I close my eyes. I don't sleep. Not really. I drift in and out, surfacing every time Missi cries or Jake shifts or the wind rattles the window. The couch is uncomfortable and the cold seeps through the quilt and my hands still smell like vinegar. But Jake is warm against my side. And Missi's cries get quieter as the night goes on—not happier, just tired. Eventually, she stops.

The silence is almost worse.

I lie there in the dark, one cat pressed against me and one cat locked away, and I wait for morning. It's going to be a long ten days.

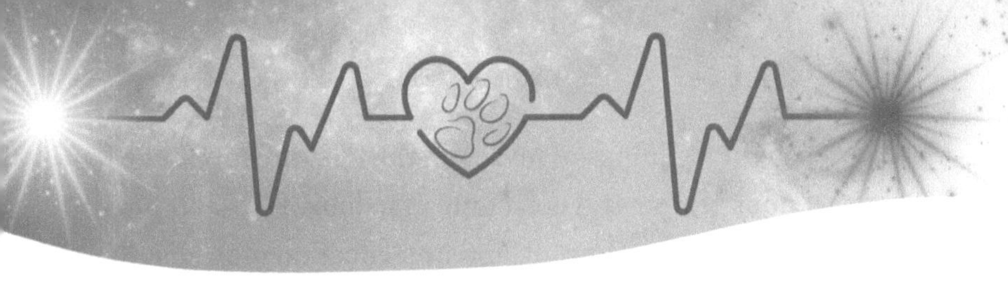

FIVE

It Spreads

MISSI

The first sore isn't alone anymore.

I am in the bedroom. I have been in the bedroom for six days. The room has become my world. The bed. The window with its view of nothing but sky. The closet door with the long mirror I've learned to avoid. The litter box in the corner, which the Witch changes every day but which still smells like confinement. Like sickness. Like me.

The door is closed. The bottom of it is stuffed with a towel so I can't even sniff the air from the rest of the house. All I can smell is bleach and my own fur and the faint iron tang that means something is still bleeding.

I noticed the second spot four days ago—just below my ear. Tender when I turned my head. I told myself it was nothing. A scratch. A bug bite. It didn't heal. Now there are more. My chin, where the fur has gone patchy and thin. The bridge of my nose, where the original sore has spread into a raw, weeping territory. And my ears.

My ears are wrong.

I caught a glimpse of myself in the long mirror on the closet door yesterday. I didn't mean to look. I was jumping down from the windowsill, and my reflection moved in the corner of my vision, and I turned. I stopped. I stared. The cat in the mirror looked like a stranger. A ragged, street-worn thing from the cold days, the hungry days. The days before home.

My ears are naked. The fur didn't just thin; it vanished. It fell out in clumps on the pillow—I wake up surrounded by pieces of myself, black and orange tufts scattered across the white cotton like something died there. The skin underneath is gray and pink and crusted with scabs. They look like raw meat. Like something chewed on and discarded.

Without the fur, the air in the room feels sharp. Every draft bites the exposed skin. Every sound feels too loud, unfiltered, ringing against the naked cartilage. I can hear the Witch moving in the kitchen, hear Jake's claws clicking on the floorboards, hear the wind against the window—all of it too close, too clear, scraping against nerves that used to be protected.

I shake my head to clear the sensation. *Bad idea.*

The scabs crack. A fresh line of heat opens up on my left ear. I feel the wetness before I feel the pain—something warm trickling down toward my jaw. I freeze, waiting for the sting to subside into the dull, rhythmic throb that is my new baseline. Everything throbs now. My face. My ears. The places where I used to be soft and whole.

Then the itch starts.

It begins deep in the ear canal. A phantom tickle. A whisper that becomes a scream. I lift my back paw. I know I shouldn't. I know the Witch will make the sad noise if she sees blood. I know it only makes things worse. I do it anyway. I scratch. The claws rake over the naked skin.

It feels horrible. It feels divine.

The doorknob turns.

I scramble off the bed, heart pounding. *Is it freedom? Is it over?*

The Witch enters. She slips in fast, pressing her leg against the frame to block the gap, and shuts the door immediately. *Click.* She does not greet me. She does not scoop me up. She does not even look at me.

She is holding The Monster.

It is the small vacuum—the loud one she uses for the curtains and the corners. She is wearing clothes I don't recognize: old sweats stained with something yellow, an apron, gloves that go up past her wrists. She smells of bleach and vinegar and something else underneath— exhaustion, maybe. Fear. The sharp, metallic smell of someone who hasn't been sleeping.

"Sorry, Missi," she mumbles. Her voice is flat. Hollow. She still doesn't look at me.

She turns The Monster on. *ROAR.*

I dive under the bed. The room vibrates. The sound fills every corner, bouncing off the walls, drilling into my naked ears until I want to scream. She is vacuuming the quilt. The pillows. The rug by the window. She is sucking up the fur I left behind—the clumps on the pillow, the scattered pieces of me that fall out every time I move. She is erasing me.

She moves methodically. Efficient. Cold. Like this is a job, not a home. Like I am a problem to be managed, not a cat to be loved. She isn't my Witch right now. She is the Jailer. She is the Cleaner. She is the one who locked me in here and comes only to scrub away the evidence that I exist.

When the noise stops, silence rushes back in, ringing in my naked ears. The absence of sound feels almost as loud as the vacuum. She pulls a bottle from her pocket. Spray. *Hiss.* The smell of bleach fills the air, choking out the vinegar, choking out everything. It burns my nose. It makes my eyes water.

She puts fresh food in my bowl. She changes the water. The bowl clinks against the floor—a familiar sound, but wrong somehow. Too clinical. Too careful.

I crawl out from under the bed. I meow. A small, broken sound. *I am here. See me. Touch me.*

She looks at me. Her eyes water. I can smell the salt before I see the tears building. She reaches a hand out— gloved, smelling of rubber and chemicals—then stops. Her fingers hover in the air between us, trembling.

"I can't," she whispers. "I can't risk it, sweetie. Just a few more days."

She stands up. She backs toward the door, still looking at me, still crying. The door opens and shuts in a heartbeat. I am alone with the bleach.

The scratching is a clock.

On the other side of the wood, Jake is waiting. He has been waiting for six days. He waits every day, all day, from the moment the Witch leaves for work until she comes home. I can hear him breathing through the gap. I can hear him shifting his weight, settling in for another vigil.

Scritch. Scritch. Pause. *Scritch.*

He doesn't meow anymore. He used to, the first few days —confused, questioning sounds that asked *why* and *when* and *please.* Now he just digs at the barrier. Steady. Patient. Like it's his job now. He knows I am in here. He doesn't understand why the pack has been split.

I go to the door. I press my nose against the towel stuffed under the frame. I inhale. The bleach is too strong. It burns. But underneath, faintly, I can smell him. Dust and warmth and the particular musk of brother. The smell of the cat who slept beside me every night of my life until six days ago.

I lie down on the floorboards. They are cold against my belly, hard against my hips. I press my naked ear against the gap at the bottom of the door—the tiny space the towel doesn't quite cover. I can hear him breathing. Slow. Steady. Waiting. *I'm here,* I tell him silently. *I'm still here.*

He scratches again. I scratch back. One paw against the wood. Weak. But there.

We lie there, separated by two inches of door, breathing

in time. Through the gap, I hear him start to purr—low and uncertain, but there. His warmth is so close. I can almost feel it through the wood. Almost.

Then, the break-in.

It happens in the evening. The light through the window has gone orange and dim. The Witch opens the door to retrieve the dinner tray, and her grip slips. The gap widens. Just a few inches. Just enough.

An orange blur shoots between her legs.

"Jake! *No!*"

He ignores her. He ignores the bleach smell, the strange chemical wrongness of the room. He sees me on the floor and he launches himself across the space between us. He is chirping, happy, desperate. He has been waiting for six days. He lands beside me. He is purring so hard his whole body vibrates. He smells like home—like the rug by the fire and the chair in the living room and everything I've been missing. He looks huge and soft and unbroken.

He leans in to groom my ear.

I snap. I don't decide to do it. It just happens. His whiskers touch the raw, naked skin and the pain explodes out of me like something that's been waiting. *Hiss. Pop.* I swipe at him. Claws out. I feel them connect—not hard, but enough.

He scrambles backward, claws skidding on the floor, eyes wide with shock. He stares at me.

He was trying to help. He was trying to clean me, to comfort me, to do the thing we've always done for each other. And I hurt him.

"Jake, out," the Witch says. Her voice is tight. Strained. She grabs him around the middle. He tenses—one last look at me, stubborn and worried—then goes limp in her arms, staring at me over her shoulder as she carries him to the door. His eyes are confused. Wounded. *Why?*

"I'm sorry, Missi. I'm sorry."

She throws him out. The door slams. The towel is shoved back into place. I am alone again.

I feel sick. He is my brother. He is the cat who nudged me forward when we were kittens in the cold. He is the only family I have left from before. And I can't let him touch me.

My skin feels wrong. It feels like something is eating me from the outside in. I am losing pieces of myself—fur and blood and the ability to be touched—one scab at a time. I am wrong. Something wrong that bites and hides. Wrong things don't get touched.

I leave the floor. It is too exposed. Too bright.

I go under the bed. It is dark here. The dust smells like old safety, like forgotten things, like the places I used to hide when I was small and scared. I fit into the darkness like I was made for it. I curl up tight. My naked ears twitch in the cold drafts from under the door.

The dark is better. The dark doesn't try to touch me.

I don't know how long I've been here when the Witch comes back.

She enters quietly. She doesn't turn on the light. She doesn't bring The Monster or the spray bottle or the gloves.

"Missi?" Her voice is soft. Tentative. She crouches by the bed, extends a hand into the darkness.

I press myself against the far wall. I don't hiss. I don't have the energy. I just... retreat.

She lies down on the floor. She flattens herself against the wood, cheek pressed to the dust, until her face is level with mine. We are inches apart. I can smell her—the vinegar still there, but weaker now, overpowered by something else. Salt. The wet smell of tears. The exhausted, wrung-out scent of someone who has been crying for a long time.

We stare at each other in the gloom.

"I know," she says. Her voice is a whisper. Hoarse. "I know it hurts. I'm sorry."

I don't answer. I just watch her. Watch the tears making tracks through the dust on her face.

"The tests came back early," she whispers. "The Healer sent a messenger." She takes a breath. It shudders in her chest. "It's not Ringworm, Missi."

She reaches a hand out, palm up, resting it on the floorboards between us. Bare skin. No glove. Her fingers are red and raw from all the washing.

"It's not Ringworm," she says again. "So I'm opening the door. You don't have to be alone anymore."

She starts to cry. Quietly. The tears drip onto the dusty floor. "They don't know what it is yet. But we go back tomorrow. We'll figure it out. I promise. We'll figure it out."

I don't move toward her hand. The sores are throbbing,

and my ears feel like they are burning, and if she touches me —if anyone touches me—I will shatter into pieces that can't be put back together.

But I don't move away.

She stays on the floor. I stay under the bed. Her hand rests between us, open and waiting and asking for nothing. The door is open. I can smell the rest of the house seeping in —the wood smoke and the herbs and the wool of the rug and the faint, lingering scent of Jake waiting in the hall. The smells of home. The smells of before.

I don't go out. Not yet. I'm not ready.

I just close my eyes and listen to her breathe. Feel her presence on the floor beside me. Let the silence settle around us like a blanket. Outside the door, Jake makes a small sound. A question. *Is it over?*

Not yet. But maybe soon.

I press my paw against the floor, toward her hand. Her fingers are cracked and red, the skin peeling from all the washing. She has been hurting too. Not touching. Just close. It's all I can give her right now.

I hope it's enough.

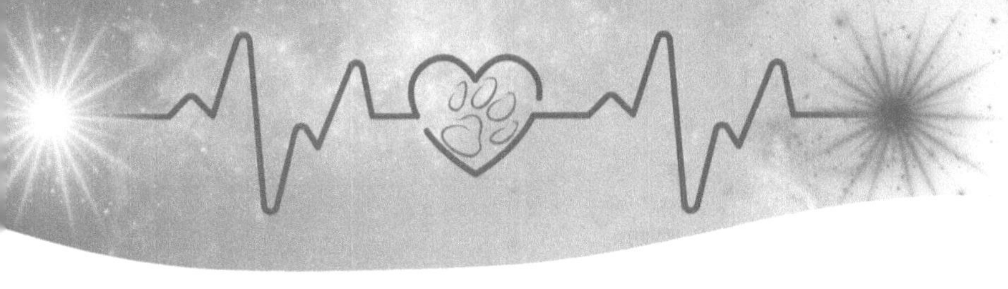

SIX

The Name

WITCH

Missi is worse.

The isolation didn't help. The vinegar didn't help. The bleach, the vacuuming, the ten days of listening to my cats cry for each other through a door—none of it helped. The Ringworm protocol was a waste of time and money and heartbreak, and now I must pay for it.

The Healer admits it on the eleventh day. "The culture is negative," she says, holding the petri dish up to the light. It grew absolutely nothing. "It's not Ringworm."

For one brief, shining moment, I feel relief. Not Ringworm. Not contagious. I can stop scrubbing my hands raw. I can stop washing everything I own. I can let Jake and Missi be together again. Then the Healer sets the dish down, and her face doesn't match the good news.

I look at Missi. She is shivering on the metal table, her ears raw and weeping, the sores on her face angrier than ever. Ten days of isolation, and she's worse, not better.

"Then what is it?"

"I don't know," the Healer says.

It is the most terrifying thing a doctor can say.

"I need to call in a Specialist," she continues. "And we need to do more tests."

More tests. More money. More time watching Missi fall apart while we chase answers that keep slipping away.

"Okay," I say. My voice sounds far away. "Whatever you need to do."

The next week is a blur of indignities.

First, the bloodwork. They have to shave a patch on Missi's front leg—what looks like her forearm—to find the vein. The clippers buzz, loud and angry, and Missi flinches at the vibration. A stripe of pale, vulnerable skin appears in the middle of her dark fur. She screams when the needle goes in. Not a yowl—a scream. High and raw and betrayed.

I have to hold her down. I press her chest against the cold metal table, feeling her heart hammer against my palm, while the Healer draws vial after vial of dark red blood from her leg. Three vials. Four. Missi's screams turn to whimpers, then to a terrible, exhausted silence.

"Almost done," the Healer murmurs. "One more."

I look at my hands, pinning down the creature I love most in the world while someone hurts her. This is for her own good. I have to believe that. The needle slides out. The

Healer presses a cotton ball to the site. Missi goes limp under my hands, panting.

"Good girl," I whisper. "Good girl. It's over."

But it isn't over. It's just beginning.

Then, the Specialist.

The Healer uses the scrying mirror in her office—a heavy silver oval mounted on the wall. I sit in the waiting room while she argues with a mage in the Capital. The walls are thin. I can hear her voice through the door, frustrated and defensive.

"Yes, I checked the liver. The enzymes are slightly elevated."

A pause. A tinny response I can't quite make out.

"Yes, the white count is elevated too. No, it doesn't fit the standard pattern. That's why I'm calling you."

Another pause. Longer.

"I understand it's expensive. But this familiar is bonded, and the witch is—yes. Yes, I'll tell her."

The door opens. The Healer looks tired. "The Specialist wants a biopsy," she says. "He won't confirm anything without tissue samples."

"Tissue samples?"

"We need to take small pieces of the affected skin. From the ears. And from the lesion above her eye."

Above her eye. I think of Missi's face. The sores spreading across her brow. Someone cutting into that.

"When?"

"Tomorrow. She'll need to be sedated."

The biopsy is worse than the blood draw.

They take her from me. "You can wait outside," the Healer says. It isn't a suggestion. "This will be easier if she doesn't smell your fear."

I want to argue. I want to say I should be there, that she needs me, that I can't just sit in the hallway while someone cuts pieces out of her face. But the Healer is already closing the door, and Missi is already gone, and I am alone in the waiting room with the toad in the glass case and the raven muttering curses under its cover.

I sit. I wait. I don't know how long it takes. Long enough that I count the tiles on the floor twice. Long enough that the raven falls silent and the toad stops pulsing and even the dust in the air seems to hold still.

I hear nothing through the door. I tell myself that's good. No screaming means she's sedated. No screaming means she isn't fighting. No screaming means she's lying on that table, eyes open and unseeing, while someone cuts into her and she doesn't even know I'm here.

The door opens. The Healer is holding her.

Missi is wrapped in a towel, limp, her head lolling against the Healer's arm. There's a cone around her neck—the plastic kind that makes cats look like sad flowers—and through the clear rim I can see the damage. One stitch on her ear. Black thread pulling the skin tight where they took a piece of her. One stitch above her eye. Right on the brow, right where the sore was the worst. The thread looks like a spider sitting on her face.

"She did well," the Healer says. "She'll be groggy for a few hours. Keep the cone on so she doesn't scratch the stitches."

I take her. She weighs nothing. She smells like blood and antiseptic and something chemical I don't recognize. Her eyes are open. Glassy. She doesn't see me.

I carry her home. Jake approaches her cautiously. He sniffs the cone, confused. He tries to groom her face and hits plastic. He sits back, ears flat, looking at me like I can explain what happened to his sister.

I can't explain anything. We wait.

Three days later, the Healer calls us back.

The message arrives by courier—a folded note with the Healer's seal. *Results in. Please come at your earliest convenience.* Earliest convenience. As if I could wait. As if I could do anything but count the hours.

I carry Missi through the streets of Miren Hollow, the carrier banging against my leg. She's still wearing the cone. The stitches come out today, the Healer said. One less indignity.

"Come with me," the Healer says when we arrive. "Let's talk in my office."

Not the exam room. The office. My stomach turns over.

The office is small and cluttered with books. It smells of old paper and dried lavender, the kind of smell that's supposed to be calming. It isn't. The Healer gestures to a chair. I sit, the carrier heavy on my lap. Missi is silent inside, exhausted from the walk, the cone making soft scraping sounds against the carrier walls.

"The biopsy results came back from the Capital," the Healer says. She taps a thick envelope on her desk. The seal is already broken. She's read it. She knows. "It confirms what the Specialist thought."

"What is it?"

She takes a breath. "It is an autoimmune condition. In familiars, we call it **The Unbinding**."

Something cold moves through my chest. Not emotion—sensation. A flicker of static along the thread that connects me to Missi, the bond I barely notice most days because it's as constant as my own heartbeat. For one horrible moment, I feel it fray. *Unbinding.* As if something is coming apart at the seams.

"In simple terms," she says, "her magic has turned against her. The energy that flows through the familiar bond, the energy that connects her to you and sustains her... it is misfiring. Instead of protecting her body, it is attacking the glue that holds her skin cells together."

I stare at her. The words make sense individually. Together, they're impossible.

"My magic is hurting her?"

"No. *Her* response to the magic is hurting her. It's a flaw in the way her body integrated with the bond. Some familiars are born with the susceptibility—it lies dormant for years, sometimes forever, until something triggers it. Stress, illness, sometimes nothing at all." She pauses. "And once it activates... it doesn't deactivate."

Doesn't deactivate.

"So..." My voice comes out thin. Wrong. "There's no cure?"

"No." She doesn't soften it. I'm grateful for that. "This is a condition that is managed, not cured. There will be flares—times when it gets worse, when the sores spread and the symptoms intensify. There will also be better times, periods where the right treatment keeps things stable."

"But it won't go away."

"No. It won't go away." She leans forward. "But we can fight it. We can give her a good life. Different than before, but good."

A good life. I hold onto that.

Then comes the list.

The Healer pulls a large amber bottle from a drawer and sets it heavily on the desk. The glass is thick, old, the kind of bottle that's been refilled a hundred times.

"We start with a systemic suppressant," she says. "It's a steroid potion. It calms the immune response, stops the body from attacking itself." She taps the glass. The liquid inside is thick and dark, almost black in the dim light of the office. "It's a heavy dose to start—we need to knock this down hard before it spreads further.

We flavored it with fish oil to mask the bitterness, but she still won't like it. You give it to her every morning, mixed into her food or straight into her mouth if she refuses to eat." She looks at me. "She'll probably refuse to eat."

I nod. *Potion. Every morning.*

She sets a small tin next to the bottle. "This is an eye balm. She scratched her cornea before we got the cone on— probably during a bad itch. This goes directly into the eye twice a day. It will sting, and she will fight you, but you have to do it. If the cornea doesn't heal, she could lose vision in that eye."

Eye balm. Twice a day. She could go blind.

"You keep her on the high dose until the skin clears," the Healer continues. "That could be two weeks, could be two months. Then, if we're lucky, we taper it down to a maintenance level. Some familiars can eventually come off the steroid entirely. Some need it for life. We won't know which one she is until we try."

"And if the steroid doesn't work?"

"Then we try something else. There are other options— stronger, with more side effects. We start with this because it's the gentlest."

Gentlest. The word feels like a joke.

"There is one more thing," the Healer says. She leans forward, and her voice shifts. Serious. "The steroid potion is hard on the body. It suppresses the immune system, which is what we want, but it also pushes the liver and kidneys to their limit. We need to check her blood every two weeks to make sure we aren't poisoning her while we're trying to save her."

I write it down. My hand moves automatically while my brain screams. *Potion. Balm. Bloodwork.*

I do the math in the margins.

Specialist Consult Fee: 10 silver.
Biopsy Lab Fee: 8 silver.
Steroid Potion: 8 silver per month.
Eye Balm: 3 silver.
Bloodwork visits: 5 silver each, recurring.

My rent is 20. My wages are 35.

I stare at the numbers. They don't work. The emergency fund is already gone from the biopsy. The specialist fee ate the rest. Now I'm looking at ongoing costs that will consume half my income, forever, on top of rent and food and the hundred small expenses of staying alive. This is an emergency. And it is also forever.

"I know it's a lot," the Healer says. Her voice is soft now, the professional distance cracking just slightly. "There are some options. Payment plans. The Temple sometimes helps with medical costs for bonded familiars. I can give you the information."

"Yes," I say. "Please."

"But we need to start the steroid today. Right now. Every day we wait is another day her body attacks itself."

I look at the bottle. The dark liquid inside. The beginning of a new life, one measured in doses and blood tests and coins I don't have.

"Okay," I say. My voice is steady. I'm proud of that. "Let's start."

The walk home is quiet.

Missi doesn't yowl. She is exhausted—from the visit, from the days of healing, from the cone she's still wearing until tomorrow. She lies in a small ball, the plastic rim catching on the blanket, and I carry her through the streets of Miren Hollow like she is made of glass.

The sun is setting. The sky is orange and pink, the kind of beautiful that feels like a cruel joke when your world is falling apart. Across the square, a young witch laughs as her familiar—a sleek gray cat—bats at her swinging braid, healthy and whole and utterly ordinary. I'm going home to give my cat medicine that might save her or might poison her, and I won't know which for weeks.

The Unbinding.

I think about the biopsy. The punch tool. The stitches pulling at her brow. I think about her lying sedated on the table, eyes open and empty, while someone cut pieces out of her. I can't tell her why.

That is the part that keeps circling in my head. I can learn the name of this thing. I can buy the potions and give the doses and take her to every blood draw. But I can't explain it to her. I can't say *This is what's wrong* and *This is why I have to put stinging medicine in your eye every day* and *This is why your body is falling apart.* She will only ever know the pain. She will only ever know that I am the one causing it.

Her body is rejecting my magic. And now her heart will reject my help. The cruelty of it is almost elegant.

I unlock the cottage door. Home. Safe. For whatever that's worth now.

I set the carrier down and open the door.

Missi emerges slowly, carefully, the cone making her clumsy. She moves with a stiffness that wasn't there two weeks ago. She limps toward her chair—*when did she start limping?*—and jumps up with visible effort, misjudging the distance because of the cone and nearly falling before she catches herself. She curls into her spot. The cone bumps the armrest, and she sighs, resting her chin on the plastic rim. The black stitch above her eye looks like a spider sitting on her brow. Her ears are scabbed and raw inside the cone's protection.

She looks at me. Small. Demanding. Broken.

Jake creeps out from behind the bookshelf. He approaches the chair cautiously, sniffing the air, trying to understand. For ten days, she was locked away. Now she's here, but she's wrong—she smells like the Healer's office, like chemicals and blood, and she's wearing this strange plastic thing that makes her look like a flower with a terrible center.

He jumps onto the chair beside her. She doesn't hiss this time. She's too tired. He studies her for a moment, then begins to groom the back of her neck—the one spot she can't reach with the cone in the way. Slow, deliberate strokes. Solving the problem he can solve. The cone bumps his head when she tries to turn toward him, and he flinches, but he doesn't leave.

I watch them. My two cats, pressed together in the chair, one broken and one bewildered.

I stand in the kitchen. The diagnosis rattles in my head. *The Unbinding. Her magic has turned against her. Managed, not cured. Forever.* I get a piece of paper. A pen. I start a list.

> *Sell the winter cloak. It's worn, but the wool is still good. Maybe 5 silver.*
> *Ask Bessa for extra shifts. Early mornings, late evenings, whatever she has.*
> *Cut food budget. Rice and beans. Oats for breakfast. No more dried fruit.*
> *Sell the silver hair comb. It was my mother's. It will break my heart. Maybe 8 silver.*
> *Ask about payment plans at the apothecary.*
> *Ask about Temple assistance.*

I write it all down. Neat. Organized. A map of the ruin. My hand cramps. I keep writing.

The light fades outside the window. The fire burns low. Missi sleeps in her chair, Jake pressed against her, the cone catching the last of the light. I look at the list. It's not enough. Even if I do all of it, the math doesn't work. There's a gap between what I have and what she needs, and I don't know how to close it.

But I have a list. I have a plan. I have something to do tomorrow, and the day after, and the day after that.

I fold the paper and put it in my pocket. Tomorrow I give her the first dose. Tomorrow we see if the steroid works. Tomorrow I start selling pieces of my life to pay for hers.

But tonight, I sit by the fire. I watch my cats sleep, tangled together, breathing in time.

Tonight, that's all I can do.

SEVEN

Potions

MISSI

There is a potion now. The Healer said it was "flavored." She lied.

Every morning, the Witch opens the amber bottle. *Click-hiss.* That sound is my signal.

I run. I don't go to my chair. I go under the sofa. I wedge myself into the farthest, darkest corner where the dust bunnies live and the air smells like forgotten things.

"Missi, please," the Witch sighs. She is on her hands and knees, her face appearing in the gap. "Don't make this harder."

I make it harder.

She has to drag me out. I hook my claws into the carpet fibers, feeling them strain and pop. I scream—a low, guttural yowl that says *I am being murdered.* She gets me into her lap. I thrash. I twist. The plastic cone bangs against her ribs. I catch her hand with a claw, drawing a thin line of red, but she doesn't let go. Her grip is iron.

She pries my jaw open. Her fingers taste like soap and skin. She squirts the sludge onto my tongue.

Dead fish. Old copper. Rot. It coats my mouth like oil, clinging to my teeth, seeping into the grooves of my tongue. I gag. I try to spit, shaking my head so hard that drool and brown liquid fly onto the inside of my cone. It splatters against the plastic, sliding down in thick streaks.

"I'm sorry," she whispers, wiping my chin with a rough cloth. "I'm so sorry."

I glare at her through the plastic wall. *You are not sorry enough.*

The medicine does something else. It hollows me out.

An hour after the sludge, a hunger tears through me. It isn't normal hunger. It is a panic. A void in my stomach that screams *FILL ME*.

I eat my breakfast. I shovel the kibble into my mouth, tilting my head sideways, scooping to get my mouth past the rim of the cone. It isn't enough. I go to Jake's bowl. He is still eating, slow and polite, crunching one piece at a time. I shove him aside. My cone hits his flank. *Move.*

He steps back, confused. He watches me inhale his food. I finish it. I lick the ceramic until it scrapes against my tongue, until there is nothing left but the ghost of flavor.

I am still hungry.

I circle the kitchen. I scream at the Witch. The sound echoes inside the cone, amplified, ringing in my own ears.

"You just ate," she says. "You had a full bowl."

You don't understand, I yell. *I am starving. The potion is eating me from the inside.*

I jump on the counter—clumsy, the cone hitting the edge, throwing off my balance. I try to tear open the bread bag. The plastic crinkles under my claws but won't give. She has to lock the food in the pantry. I sit outside the door and cry because I am empty, because my stomach is a hole that nothing fills.

Then comes the thirst.

I drink until my stomach sloshes. I dip my head into the bowl, the cone acting like a funnel, scooping up water that washes down my neck. My chest fur is soaked, the cold spreading through the hair to the skin beneath. I shake myself dry, and the wet plastic smacks against my ears. *Thwack-thwack-thwack.* Water droplets spray across the floor. I drink the bowl dry. I stand by the sink and yell until she refills it.

And because I drink, I pee.

The litter box is the final indignity. I step in. The clay is cool and gritty under my paws. I lower my head to sniff— the law of the box—and the cone scoops up a rim-full of dirty litter. I jerk my head up. Gravel rains down on my face. It slides down the plastic funnel and settles around my neck, gritty and sharp against my fur. And the clumps... they are huge. Heavy. The box is a swamp.

I try to bury my business, but the cone hits the high sides of the box. *Scrape. Scrape.* I can't see where I'm digging. I step in wet clay, feel it squeeze between my toes. I leave the box with litter trapped in my collar, rattling against my throat with every step.

I am a Queen. And I have become a garbage collector.

I feel dirty.

This is the worst part. Worse than the hunger, worse than the cone. I cannot reach my back. I cannot reach my tail. My fur feels greasy. The natural oils are building up, turning my coat into heavy, separated spikes. Dust settles on me, and I cannot lick it off. I can smell myself—stale, musty, wrong.

I itch. Not the sores—the *fur*.

I try to groom. I turn my head, extending my tongue. *Lick.* I lick the inside of the plastic cone. It tastes like dust and old saliva and the residue of brown medicine. I try again. *Scrape.* My tongue drags uselessly against plastic.

I rub my side against the corner of the wall. Hard. Trying to scrape the dirty feeling off. It doesn't work. The wall doesn't care. The dirt remains. I look like a stray. I smell like a stray. I was supposed to be done with that life. The memory comes unbidden—matted fur in the cold, the smell of motor oil, the engine that burned my tail. Siblings who didn't make it out of the dark.

I decide I am done.

I am lying on the rug, the plastic rim pressing into my throat. The itch under the collar is maddening—a crawling, tickling sensation I cannot reach.

I lift my back leg. I wedge it inside the cone. I push.

The plastic digs into my jaw. It hurts. I don't care. I push harder. I hook my claws over the fabric loops that tie it to my neck. I feel the threads strain. I strain. My neck stretches. My eyes bulge.

Pop.

The knot gives. The cone slides over my ears—Loss catches the raw edge of the left one, and I hiss at the sting—but then it's past, it's gone, it hits the floor with a hollow clatter.

Air.

Cool, beautiful air hits my neck. I shake my head—truly shake it, with no weight, no plastic thunder. My ears flap. My whiskers spread wide.

I immediately start to groom. My neck is sweaty and matted, the fur pressed flat in strange directions. I lick it smooth. I groom my shoulder. I groom my flank. I groom until my tongue is dry and my coat lies right again.

"Missi?"

The Witch stands in the doorway. She looks at the cone on the floor. She looks at me.

"Oh, Missi. No."

She picks up the cone. I run.

It takes her ten minutes to catch me. It takes five minutes to tie it back on. She uses a double knot this time, pulling it tight. "Please keep it on," she begs. "You'll scratch the stitches."

I stare at her. She does not understand. The stitches are not the problem. The *everything* is the problem.

An hour later, while she is washing dishes, I do it again. *Push. Strain. Pop.*

She finds me asleep in the chair, the cone lying on the floor like a dead enemy. She sighs. She picks it up. She looks at my exhausted face, my ears finally free, my body finally at peace. She puts the cone on the table.

"Fine," she says. "Just... while I'm watching you. You can have a break."

I rest my chin on my paws. I won.

The afternoon is mine.

I spend it in the chair, grooming properly for the first time in days. My neck. My shoulders. The base of my tail. The Witch watches me from the kitchen, but she doesn't move. She lets me have this.

It almost feels normal. Almost feels like before.

Then the light changes. The sun dips. And the Witch reaches for the small tube on the counter.

The evening is for the Eye. This, I cannot escape.

The stitch above my left eye is tight. The skin around it is angry and hot. She sits me on the table. She holds my head steady, her thumb pressing gently into my cheek.

"Ready?"

I am never ready.

She pulls my eyelid back. I feel the air hit the wet surface of my eye. The tube comes down. A blob of thick, greasy ointment drops directly onto the exposed tissue. It spreads over my vision, turning the room into a smeared, oily blur. It stings—a sharp chemical bite that makes my eye water, makes me want to dig my paw in and scrub it clean.

I raise my paw to do exactly that. *Thwack.* The cone is back. My paw hits plastic.

"I can't trust you," she says, checking the knot, making it tighter than before. "I'm sorry."

The plastic world returns. I jump down from the table. I stumble, my depth perception gone, my head in a bucket, my mouth tasting of fish-oil poison, my eye streaming tears through a layer of grease, my stomach screaming for food I don't need.

This is my life now.

Jake has been watching.

He approaches me on the rug. He sees the cone is back. He doesn't run. He doesn't flinch. He leans in. He doesn't try to groom my face—he knows better now. He sticks to the shoulder blades. The safe zone. He used to always start with the ears. He has learned the new map of me—where the pain lives and where the safe country begins.

His tongue rasps against my fur, steady and warm. He finds the places I can't reach, the places the cone steals from me.

I lean into him. My plastic wall bumps his nose. He doesn't move away. I press my plastic rim against his side. I close my stinging eye, let the tears soak into his fur.

I am tired of fighting. I am tired of eating sludge and being a shovel and living inside a bucket. But I am still here. Jake is still here. The Witch is still here, washing dishes, pretending she isn't watching us.

And tomorrow, I will try to take the cone off again.

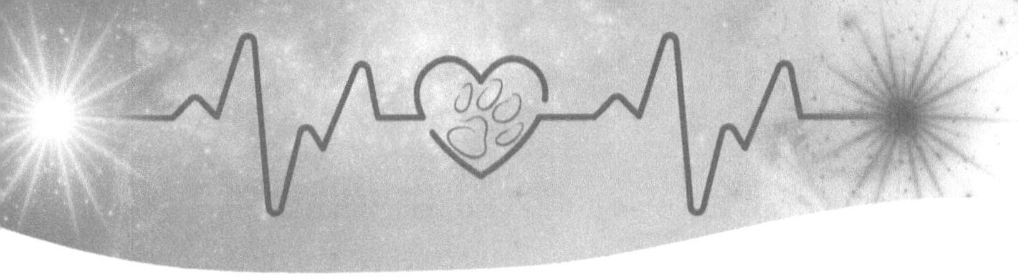

EIGHT

Hope

WITCH

Two weeks.

I count the days like a miser counts coins. Fourteen mornings of the full dose—Missi clamped between my knees, the cone knocking against my ribs, the amber sludge forced down her throat while she gags and glares and promises retribution. Fourteen evenings of the eye balm, holding her head steady while she squirms, watching the ointment spread across her vision. Fourteen nights of checking her face before bed, looking for redness, looking for blood, looking for any sign that it's getting worse.

I watch her obsessively. Every glance is an audit. Every time she moves, I track her paws, ready to intervene if they go toward her face.

Is it better?

The sores are gone. Not just better. *Gone.* The scabs have fallen off, leaving behind pink, shiny skin that looks raw but isn't—it's healing. New skin. Clean skin. And on the tips of her ears, where the velvet used to be, where the flesh was naked and weeping, there is a ghost of white fuzz returning. The redness has cooled. The heat that radiated from her skin for weeks—the low fever I could feel just by holding my hand near her face—has vanished.

I stand over her chair in the morning light, looking at her ears, her chin, the bridge of her nose where this all started. The craters are filling in. The landscape of her face is smoothing out. I tell myself not to hope. Hope is dangerous when you're two weeks into a treatment that might take months. Hope sets you up for the fall.

But the red is gone. The fuzz is growing. She's eating without screaming, sleeping without scratching.

I hope anyway.

We go back to the Healer on day fifteen.

The walk there is different this time. Missi still yowls in the carrier—she'll never forgive me for that indignity—but my chest isn't tight with dread. I'm not bracing for bad news. I'm almost... eager.

The Healer lifts the cone. She inspects the ears, tilting Missi's head gently to catch the light. She inspects the chin. She runs her fingers along the bridge of Missi's nose. She smiles. It is the first time I have seen her smile in a month.

"She looks fantastic," the Healer says. "The skin is quiet. The inflammation is down. And look—" She touches Missi's ear, where the white fuzz has grown in thick enough to see. "The hair is cycling back. That's an excellent sign."

I reach out. My fingers brush the new fur—soft as down, impossibly delicate. Alive. "So she's cured?"

The word comes out before I can stop it. I know better. The Healer told me—*managed, not cured.* But looking at Missi's ears, seeing the fur return, it's hard not to believe.

"No," the Healer says gently. "She is suppressed. The medicine is holding the wall up. Now, we have to see if the wall can stand on its own."

She pulls out a fresh sheet of paper and writes out a new schedule.

WEEK 3: REDUCE DOSE BY 25%. FROM 1.0 TO 0.75.

WEEK 4: REDUCE TO HALF DOSE. FROM 0.75 TO 0.5.

GOAL: FIND THE LOWEST EFFECTIVE DOSE.

"We go slow," the Healer says. "If you see pinkness, if you see her scratch, we go back up. But if she stays clear..." She taps the paper. "We can try taking the cone off."

My heart jumps. "Now?"

"Do it in stages. An hour in the evening while you watch her. If she scratches, it goes back on. She needs to relearn that she doesn't itch."

I fold the paper and tuck it in my pocket, next to the list of things I'm selling to pay for this. For the first time, that list doesn't feel like a funeral inventory. It feels like an investment.

That evening, the cottage is quiet.

Jake is curled on the rug by the fire, watching me with his usual wariness. Missi is in her chair, the cone resting on her paws, waiting for whatever indignity comes next. I put the amber bottle on the table. I look at the syringe.

Usually, I draw it to the **1.0** line. Full dose. Tonight, I draw it to **0.75**. It looks like too little. It looks like a mistake. My hand hovers over the bottle, wanting to add more, wanting to be safe. *Trust the math,* I tell myself. *Trust the Healer.*

I give Missi the smaller dose. She swallows it, tensing for the usual assault on her senses, and blinks when it's over so fast. She looks almost confused—like she was prepared for a war and got a skirmish.

"Good girl," I murmur. "Now the big test."

I sit on the floor next to the chair. Jake's ears perk up. He knows something is happening. My hands shake as I reach for the knot at Missi's neck.

"Don't scratch," I beg her. "Please, Missi. Be smart. Show me you don't need this anymore."

I untie the gauze loops. The knot falls away. The cone slides off.

Missi freezes. For a moment, she doesn't move—just sits there, head free, like she's forgotten what to do without the plastic prison. Then she shakes. A violent, full-body rattle that starts at her ears and ends at her tail. Her whole body shivers with the relief of it.

She looks at me. *Is it real?*

"It's real. For now. Don't make me regret it."

She immediately bends in half. She grooms her shoulder, making a low, guttural sound of satisfaction. She grooms her flank. She grooms the base of her tail, her tongue working furiously over the spots she hasn't reached in weeks.

I watch her like a hawk. My muscles are coiled, ready to grab her if her paw goes toward her face. Her back leg comes up.

"No!" I lunge forward.

Missi freezes, paw mid-air. She looks at me, offended. She isn't scratching. She is just grooming her toes. I sink back onto my heels. My heart is hammering against my ribs.

"Sorry," I whisper. "Sorry. I'm just... watching."

She gives me a look of pure disdain and goes back to cleaning her toes.

She grooms for an hour. Methodically, thoroughly, reclaiming every inch of herself. Then, exhausted and fluffy and smelling like herself instead of plastic and medicine, she curls up on the rug beside Jake. I sit there for another hour, just watching her sleep. Every time her ear twitches, I flinch. But she doesn't wake up. She doesn't scratch.

I put the cone back on for the night—just to be safe— and she doesn't fight me. She's too tired, too satisfied. The rules have changed, and she knows it.

Week three is a holding pattern.

Day 18: Dose 0.75. Ears look good. Fuzz is getting thicker, soft as down. **Day 20:** Dose 0.75. No redness. No scratching. The cone stays off during the day now. I only put it on when I leave for work, and even then, she gives me a look that says *I'm tolerating this, but my patience has limits.*

Then, the reunion.

I'm in the kitchen, washing the syringe, when I hear a soft chirping sound from the living room. Not Missi's demanding yowl—something softer. An invitation. I peek around the corner.

Missi is lying on the rug, cone-free. Jake is lying next to her, close but not touching, the way he's learned to be these past weeks. For so long, Jake has been careful. He has groomed her shoulders, her back, the safe zones. He has avoided her face like it was made of glass.

Now, slowly, he leans in. He extends his tongue. He licks her ear.

I hold my breath. *Don't snap, Missi. Don't hurt him. Please.* She leans into it.

She tilts her head, offering him the very spot that was raw meat three weeks ago. Jake washes her ear with long, slow strokes. He washes her chin. He washes the white fuzz on her nose, the place where the first sore appeared, the place where this all started. He is reclaiming her. Washing away the smell of the sickness, the plastic, the medicine. Making her his sister again.

Missi closes her eyes. A sound starts in her chest—the purr, the real purr, not the rusty broken thing from before. I feel it in my own chest. Not sound—something deeper. The thread between us, the one that flickered with static when the Healer said *Unbinding*, goes warm and steady.

I lean against the doorframe. I press my hand over my mouth so I don't make a sound. I cry into the dishtowel so I don't disturb them.

Day 21: We go to 0.5. Half dose.

This is the scary one. Half the medicine. Half the protection. The Healer warned me—this is where we find out if the wall stands on its own. I draw the syringe to the 0.5 line. It barely looks like anything. A few drops of amber liquid.

Missi swallows it and barely seems to notice. The hunger is fading—she doesn't scream at the pantry door anymore, doesn't steal Jake's food. She's turning back into herself.

The Apothecary greets me by name when I come for the refill. "We're tapering," I tell him. "Half dose now."

"That's excellent news," he says, wrapping the bottle in brown paper. "That means this will last twice as long."

I almost laugh. I'd forgotten about the money. I'd been

so focused on the ears, the skin, the cone, the fear. "Yes," I say. "Good for the budget."

I buy a small piece of chicken from the grocer on the way home. Just a breast, nothing fancy. I poach it for Missi. A celebration.

We sit by the fire that night—me in my chair, Missi in hers, Jake on the rug between us. She eats her chicken with delicate, precise bites. I eat my rice and beans. The cone is in the closet. The medicine is fading. I pull out the book I borrowed from the lending library. The chapter on *Remission.*

"Long-term management is possible," the text says. "With careful monitoring, many familiars live symptom-free for months or years at a time."

Months or years.

I look at Missi. She's grooming her paw, her ears soft with new fur, her face smooth and healed. She looks like herself again. She looks like the cat I had before all this started. Maybe by winter, we'll have a rhythm. Maybe I can finally fix the draft in the bedroom window. Maybe—

Day 24: I see the pink.

It's morning. I'm filling the syringe—0.5, half dose, the amount that's been working—when Missi turns her head and the light catches her ear. There's a spot. Small. Easy to miss. But I've been staring at her face for a month. I know every centimeter of her skin.

Pink. Just a flush of color at the edge of her ear, where the new fur is thinnest.

My hands go still. *It's nothing,* I tell myself. *She probably just scratched it in her sleep. It's irritation. It's nothing.*

I give her the dose. I watch her all morning.

By afternoon, she's scratching. Not frantically—not the desperate, bloody digging from before. Just a paw lifted to her ear, a quick rake of claws over the spot that wasn't there yesterday.

"No," I whisper. "No, no, no."

I grab her paw. She looks at me, annoyed. The pink spot is redder now. And beside it, barely visible, the skin is starting to flake.

My stomach drops. My hands go cold around her paw. I sit on the floor with my cat in my lap. She squirms, wanting to scratch, wanting to reach the itch that's come back. Half dose isn't enough. The wall isn't holding.

I close my eyes. The hope I'd been building, carefully, brick by brick—I feel it start to crumble.

Tomorrow, I call the Healer. Tomorrow, we go back up. Tonight, I hold Missi and try not to cry.

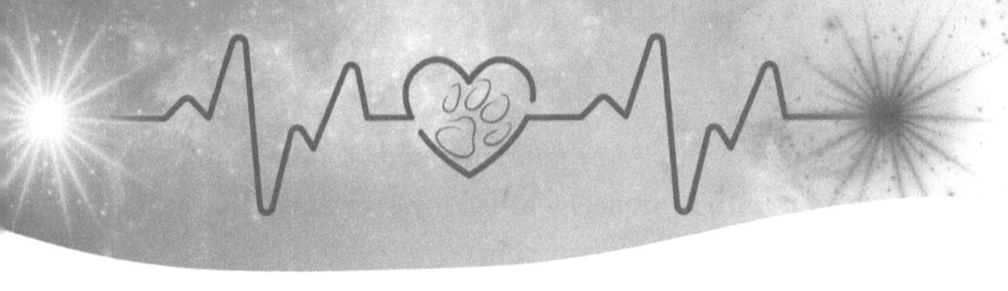

NINE

Not Working

MISSI

I won. I don't know how, and I don't care why. I won.

The scabs dried up. They turned into hard, crusty little shields that fell off one by one, leaving behind skin that was pink and smooth and new. Then came the fuzz. Soft, white velvet began to cover my naked ears. It didn't itch. It didn't burn. It just grew, reclaiming the territory I had lost.

The Witch was so happy. She cried, but they were the good kind of tears—the kind that smell like salt and relief, not fear. She took the cone off. She put it in the closet. She closed the door.

Air.

I shook my head. I groomed my shoulder. I groomed my tail. I walked through the house without bumping into door frames. I was small again. I was sleek. I was *me*.

For three days, I was the Queen of the Cottage again.

I remember those days perfectly. The sun was brighter. The rug was softer. I spent an entire afternoon on the windowsill, just feeling the air move past my whiskers. I groomed my face—my poor, battered face—washing the new fur until it shone. I washed my ears, marveling at the lack of pain. I washed my chin.

Jake joined me. We slept in a pile on the rug, orange and tuxedo, a tangle of limbs and purrs. He licked the top of my head, and I didn't flinch. I leaned into him. I was warm, and I was whole, and the burning had stopped.

I chased a moth in the kitchen. I leaped from the floor to the counter in a single fluid motion, paws barely tapping the wood. The Witch didn't scold me. She clapped.

"Look at you," she whispered, her eyes shining. "You're back."

I was back. I was *fast*.

Then came the Taper.

The Witch explained it to me while she prepared the morning dropper. "We're going down to the half-dose, Missi," she said. Her voice was light, but her hands were careful. "You're doing so well. We don't need the big guns anymore."

She drew the amber liquid up. Half the amount. I watched the glass tube. Usually, I hate the sight of it. Today, it meant less poison. Less time pinned in her lap.

She gave it to me. It still tasted like copper and dead fish, but there was less of it. I swallowed it without a fight. I didn't even run to my chair afterward. I sat on the rug and cleaned my paws, arrogant in my health. *See?* I thought. *I beat it. I survived the poison, and now the punishment is ending.*

That was Day One of the half-dose. It was a perfect day. I ate my dinner—the hunger was fading, too, settling back into a normal appetite. I slept at the foot of the Witch's bed, guarding her feet, purring deep in my throat.

Day Two was good, too. I felt a little tired in the afternoon. A heaviness in my limbs. I told myself it was just a good nap. I told myself I was catching up on all the sleep I missed when the cone was banging against my head.

I woke up, stretched, and groomed my ears. They felt… warm. Not hot. Just warm. The same warmth I felt the day before the first sore opened—back when I thought it was nothing, back when I was still whole. I had been in the shade.

I ignored it.

Day Three.

I woke up with a twitch. It wasn't a pain. It was a suggestion. A whisper from somewhere inside my own skin. *We were never really gone.*

I shook my head. *No.*

I rubbed my ear against the cool leg of the table. The sensation went away. See? Just a regular itch. A dust mite. A stray hair. Nothing.

I went to the kitchen for breakfast. The Witch was happy. She hummed as she filled my bowl. "Half-dose day three," she said, scratching my spine. "You look great, Missi."

I accepted the praise. I *did* look great.

But as I ate, I felt it again. A prickle on my chin. I paused, kibble in my mouth. I waited. It faded. *Just dry skin,* I told myself. *The new fur is growing in. It tickles.*

I finished my breakfast. I went to the window. The sun didn't feel as good today. It felt too hot. It made the skin on my face feel tight. I moved to the shade under the table.

Jake came to see me. He bumped his nose against my shoulder. *Play?*

I looked at him. I felt a flash of irritation—sharp and sudden. *Don't touch me.*

I didn't hiss. I just stood up and walked away. I needed space. I needed the air to stop touching me.

Day Four.

I couldn't lie to myself anymore.

I woke up in the gray light of dawn, and I knew before I opened my eyes. My face was throbbing. Not the dull ache of healing. The sharp, rhythmic pulse of active war.

I raised a paw. I touched my left ear. Wet. I pulled my paw away. My ears flattened on their own. Even in the dim light, I could see the dark smear on my white fur.

I hadn't scratched it. I swear I hadn't scratched it. The sore had just... opened. The medicine stopped, and the burning came back. That simple. That fast.

I sat up. The movement pulled at the skin above my eye. *Sting.* I closed my eyes. I felt the map of my face redrawing itself in lines of fire. The chin. The ear. The brow.

The burning was back. Worse than before. The eye was quiet. For now.

The Witch puts food in front of me.

The good food. The wet food she saves for special occasions, the kind that usually makes me come running from wherever I am in the house. It smells like fish and fat. I look at it. I look away.

"Missi?" Her voice is worried. It's always worried now. "You need to eat something, sweetheart."

I don't want to eat. Eating means lifting my head. Eating means chewing. Chewing stretches the skin on my chin, and the skin on my chin is raw meat again.

I stay where I am, curled in my chair. The cushion is the same. The shape of it still holds me. But my body doesn't settle. I shift positions. Shift again. Every angle presses something raw against the fabric. I look at the closet door. I know the cone is in there. I know the full bottle is in there. I know what comes next.

The Witch takes the food away. I hear her in the kitchen, the soft sounds of her moving, the long pause that means she's standing still and thinking. She hasn't seen the ear yet. She hasn't seen the blood. But she knows. She feels the heavy silence in the house.

I should go to her. I should force down a few bites, show her I'm okay.

I'm not okay. I don't have the energy to pretend. I close my eyes. The darkness behind them is the only place that doesn't hurt.

Jake comes to find me.

He enters the room cautiously. He knows the mood has changed. The air in the cottage is thick with disappointment. He approaches my chair. He puts his face near mine. *I'm here,* his eyes say. *I love you. Let me wash the bad smell away.*

I hiss at him.

It's not a warning. It's real—lips pulled back, scabs stretching, a sound that comes from the bottom of my lungs. *Get away.*

He freezes. I swipe at him. Not hard. Not with claws. But enough to make him scramble backward, enough to put space between us.

He retreats to the corner by the bookshelf. He tucks his tail around his nose. He watches me with that wounded confusion, and something cold curls in my belly. The urge to groom him rises—and I have to swallow it down.

I feel guilty immediately. He is my brother. We were a pile of cats just two days ago. But I also feel like my skin is on fire. Like I am caught in a thunderstorm and he is chirping about a sunbeam. I can't explain it. I don't have words. I just have this anger. This fear. The itch that came back when I thought it was gone.

Jake stays in his corner. I stay in my chair. The space between us is three body-lengths. It feels farther.

I can't be here anymore.

Not in the chair, not in the open, not where the Witch keeps looking at me and Jake keeps watching me.

I climb down from the chair. My legs feel weak. The sores on my paws aren't back yet—thank the stars—but I walk like they are. I walk like an old cat carrying a heavy load.

The bookshelf. There's a gap behind it, a dark space where the wood meets the wall. I haven't been back there since the first week. I squeeze into the gap. It is tight. Dust bunnies brush against my raw chin. I fit. Barely.

The darkness is cool. It doesn't ask anything of me. No one can see me here. No one expects me to act healthy here. I can just exist, small and hidden and broken.

I wait. I wait for the Witch to find me. I wait for the "Oh no." I wait for the carrier.

It came back. It always comes back.

I curl up as small as I can make myself. The burning is patient. I am not.

TEN

Back to the Healer

WITCH

The carrier is heavy again.

I lift it off the floor. Missi is silent inside. She doesn't fight me this time. She walked right into it, tail tucked, head low, like she knows this is just where she lives now.

I look at the bookshelf. There are tufts of white fur caught in the gap where she was hiding. Dried blood on the floorboards. We failed. I don't say it out loud. I don't need to. The silence in the cottage screams it. The Taper was a mistake. The hope was a mistake.

I put on my coat. My hands fumble with the buttons— three tries to get them through the holes. I slept maybe two hours last night, lying on the floor next to the bed, listening to Missi breathe. It's raining outside. A cold, gray drizzle that hasn't stopped in days.

I lock the door. We go back to the Healer.

The Healer doesn't smile today.

She lifts Missi onto the metal table. She checks the eye first—still clear, thank the stars—then moves to the ears. She inspects the wet left one, tilting Missi's head toward the light. She inspects the raw chin.

"It happens," she says quietly. She isn't dismissive; she sounds tired. "With autoimmune conditions, the first attempt is often... optimistic. We tried to hold the wall up with just the steroid. The wall fell."

I nod. I should ask questions. I should be taking notes. But the words keep sliding past me, and I have to concentrate just to stay standing.

"So we go back to the full dose?" I ask.

"Yes. Back to 1.0 on the steroid. Immediately."

She reaches into the cabinet. She bypasses the amber bottles. She pulls out a box I haven't seen before. Inside is a small bottle of clear, thick oil.

"And we add this," she says. "This is the Second Wall."

"What is it?"

"It's a modulator. It works differently than the steroid. The steroid suppresses everything—the whole immune response, good and bad. This targets the specific cells that are attacking her skin. It's stronger. More precise." She sets it on the table. "It takes time. Two weeks, maybe three, before it builds up enough in her system to hold the line on its own. Until then, we keep the steroid high. Once the modulator is established..." She pauses. "We can try tapering the steroid again. Slower this time. The goal is to get her off the steroid entirely, or at least down to a minimal dose. The modulator does the heavy lifting. The steroid just bridges the gap until it kicks in."

Two weeks. Three. More poison. More of this.

"And if it doesn't work?"

"Then we try something else." The Healer's voice is steady. Patient. She has had this conversation before. "There are always options. They just get harder."

She picks up the bottle again, turning it so I can see the label. "It is also... difficult."

"Difficult how?"

"It tastes vile," the Healer says bluntly. "Worse than the steroid. And the texture is oily. Most familiars react poorly to it. They drool. They foam." She meets my eyes. "I need to be honest with you. This part is hard on the owner. You will feel like you are poisoning her. You will have to hold her through what looks like a seizure. It's just the taste response —it's not hurting her—but it doesn't look that way. Many people struggle with it."

They foam.

I look at Missi. She is pressed flat against the metal table, making herself as small as possible. I have done this to her. Every day for weeks, I have held her down and forced poison into her mouth, and now I'm going to do something worse.

"But it works?"

"It's our best shot," she says. "Combined with the steroid, this gives us the highest chance of putting the fire out for good."

She pauses. Sets the bottle down between us. "It's also expensive. Forty silver a bottle."

Forty silver. That is my rent for two months.

I look at the bottle. I look at Missi.

"Okay," I say. My voice is steady. I'm proud of that. "Give it to me."

I don't check my purse. I don't check the ledger in my head. If I check, I'll hesitate. And I can't hesitate.

At home, I prepare for the evening ritual.

I read the Healer's instructions three times. The words blur together; I have to mouth them to make them stick. I set out the towel, the tissues, the liver treats for after. I fill a small bowl with water in case she needs to rinse the taste. I put on my oldest shirt—the one with the stains that won't wash out.

I tell myself this is medicine. I tell myself she'll forgive me.

I sit at the table and wait for evening. I should eat something. I should rest. Instead, I watch the light move across the floor and try not to think about the foam.

First, the Steroid. Back to 1.0. Missi knows this one. She hates it, but she swallows the fishy sludge with grim resignation. One enemy she's learned to tolerate.

Then, the new one.

I shake the bottle. I draw up the clear oil. It smells like rancid chemicals—sharp, medicinal, wrong. I hold Missi tight. I have wrapped her in a towel—a "burrito," the Healer called it—so she can't claw me. She is tense against my chest, body rigid. Her nose twitches toward the bottle.

"I'm sorry," I whisper. "I'm so sorry."

My hands are shaking. I have to grip the syringe harder to keep it steady.

I squirt the oil into her mouth.

The reaction is instant. Missi gags. She throws her head back. She doesn't swallow; she shakes her head violently, spraying droplets of oil onto my shirt, onto my face, onto the wall behind me.

Then comes the foam.

Thick, white bubbles erupt from her lips. Long, stringy ropes of saliva hang from her jaw, dripping onto the towel, onto her paws, onto the floor. She is drooling like a rabid beast, her mouth working frantically to get the taste out. Her eyes are huge, whites showing. Her body convulses with each gag.

"It's okay!" I grab a tissue. I try to wipe her mouth, but the foam keeps coming. "It's just the taste, Missi! It's okay!"

She wrenches free from the towel. She runs.

She runs to the rug and drags her face across it, leaving a snail-trail of slime. She runs to the kitchen and shakes her head, flinging white foam onto the cabinets. She runs in circles, gagging, pawing at her mouth.

I stand there, the empty syringe in my hand.

I did this. I held her down and I did this to her. The Healer called it a taste response. It looks like a seizure. She said it looks worse than it is. It looks like torture. She promised it works. I watch my cat drag her face across the floor, and I pray she wasn't lying.

This is what helping looks like. This is what love looks like. This is what I have to do every single day for the next two weeks, maybe three, maybe longer.

I smell the oil on my fingers. I go to the sink. I wash my hands. I wash them again. The smell won't come off.

The house is quiet.

Missi is hiding under the bed. I checked on her ten minutes ago; the drooling has stopped, but she won't look at me. She pressed herself against the far wall, as far from my reaching hand as she could get. I don't blame her. I wouldn't look at me either.

Jake is sitting outside the bedroom door, guarding it. He hasn't moved in an hour. Every few minutes, he makes a small sound—not a meow, just a chirp. A question directed at the gap under the door. She doesn't answer him either.

I sit at the kitchen table. The ledger is open. The candle is burning low. I should have eaten today. I didn't. The thought of food makes my stomach turn. Every time I close my eyes, I see the foam.

I dip my pen.

Steroid Refill: 8 silver.
New Modulator: 40 silver.
Healer Visit: 5 silver.
Total: 53 silver.

My monthly wage is 35.

I stare at the numbers. They just sit there. They don't care that they're impossible. I look at the "Expenses" column.

I draw a line through *Food (Human)*. I draw a line through *Heat*.

Rent.
~~*Food (Human).*~~
Food (Cat).
~~*Heat.*~~
Debt.

It's late spring. I can sleep in my coat. I have a bag of rice. I can forage for greens in the garden.

It's not enough.

I look around the cottage. The silver hair comb. It belonged to my grandmother. She wore it on her wedding day, and her mother wore it before that. It's heavy. Real silver. I haven't worn it in years—I have nowhere to wear it—but I take it out sometimes. Just to hold. *Estimate: 15 silver.*

The winter cloak. The one I patched last month, proud of the neat stitches. Good wool. Warm wool. The kind of cloak that gets you through a hard winter without shivering.

Bessa at the store might buy it back, if she's feeling generous. *Estimate: 10 silver.*

The extra shifts. Bessa needs help with inventory. I can work nights. I can work weekends. I don't need to sleep.

I write it all down.

Sell comb.
Sell cloak.
Night shifts.

It balances. Barely. If nothing breaks. If I don't eat meat. If I don't get sick. If the modulator works and we don't have to try something harder. Something more expensive.

I put the pen down.

A tear hits the ledger. It smears the ink on the word *Rent.* I wipe it away with my thumb.

"Stop it," I whisper to the empty room.

I sit there, shaking, my hand pressed over my mouth to keep the sound in. I let the tears come for a minute, but then force myself to stop. Tears are a luxury. I have rent to pay. I wipe my face on my sleeve. I close the ledger.

I am so tired. I am so tired of being the one who hurts her. I am so tired of watching her run from me. I am so tired of doing the right thing when the right thing looks exactly like cruelty.

But tired doesn't matter. Tired doesn't get to win.

I stand up. I walk to the bedroom. Jake is still at the door. As I watch, he noses something across the floor—the velvet catnip mouse, the one I bought him months ago. He pushes it under the gap with his paw, then sits back and waits. She doesn't take it. But he tried.

"I know, buddy," I murmur. "She's mad at both of us right now."

I step over him carefully. I open the door just enough to slip through, then close it behind me so he can't follow. The Healer said to give her space after the first dose. Let her calm down. Don't crowd her.

I lie down on the floor next to the bed. The wood is hard and cold against my hip. I can hear Missi breathing underneath—fast, shallow, pressed against the far wall.

"We try again tomorrow," I whisper to the dust ruffle. "And the day after that. And the day after that. Two weeks, the Healer said. Maybe three. Then it gets easier."

I don't know if I'm talking to her or to myself.

She doesn't answer. But she is there. And she is alive.

Everything else is negotiable.

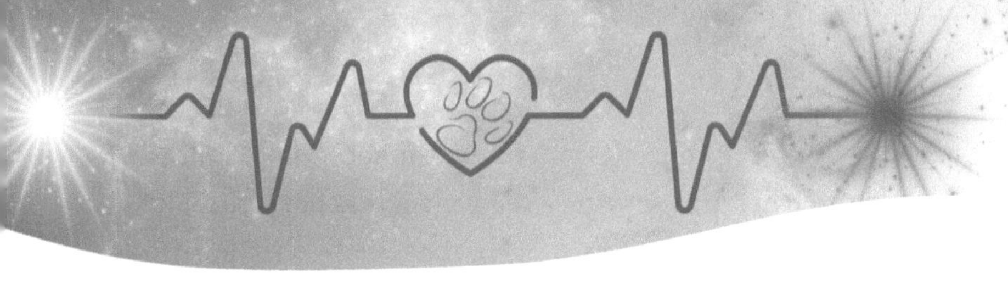

The Oil and the Fire

MISSI

There is a new poison.

The Witch calls it "The Oil." The amber sludge was bad —it tasted like dead fish. But this? This is clear. It looks like water. It is a trap.

The evening ritual is no longer a treatment. It is a hunt.

I know the signs. The sun goes down. The Witch closes the curtains. She moves the chair away from the table and takes a deep breath, the kind you take before you dive into cold water. That is my signal.

I run.

I don't just walk away; I bolt. I scramble under the sofa, hooking my claws into the carpet to pull myself deep into the shadows. I squeeze behind the wood stove. I climb to the top of the cabinets where she needs a chair to reach me.

"Missi, please," she begs. Her voice is already thick with tears. "Please don't make me chase you."

I make her chase me. I have to. The instinct to survive is stronger than my love for her.

She drags me out from under the sofa. I hiss. I thrash. I scratch her arm, leaving a red welt across her wrist. She doesn't let go. She wraps me in the towel—the "Burrito"—trapping my legs, trapping my claws, and pins me against her chest.

She is crying. I can feel her chest hitching against my back. Her tears drip onto my head, cold and wet on my fur.

"I'm sorry," she sobs. "I'm so sorry, baby."

She pries my jaw open. Her hands are shaking. She squirts the clear liquid onto my tongue, and it tastes like fire —like rotting lemons and chemical burn.

My body rejects it instantly. I don't decide to do it; it just happens. My mouth floods with saliva. Thick, white foam erupts from my lips, bubbling up, choking me, stringing from my jaw like I am a rabid beast. I shake my head violently, spraying foam onto the Witch's face, mixing with her tears.

She wipes my mouth with a cloth that immediately becomes slimy. I wrench free from the towel.

I run. I slide across the floor on my own drool. I rub my face against the rug, trying to scrape the taste out of my mouth, but it lingers. It coats my throat. This is my life now. She chases. I run. She catch

The days blur together. One. Two. Five. The hunt changes, but the ending never does.

Day Three, I wedge myself behind the wood stove. The

gap is tight, barely wider than my shoulders. This used to be a place of warmth and safety, where I would nap on the hearthstones. Now it is just a trench in a war. The Witch has to move the whole stove to reach me—I hear her grunting, the scrape of iron on stone. She burns her hand on the metal. I smell singed skin. She catches me anyway.

Day Six, I make it to the top of the bookshelf. She has to drag the kitchen chair across the room, climb up, and pry me off the wood while I cling with all four sets of claws. A book falls. Then another. She doesn't stop.

Day Nine, I try the bedroom. Under the bed, the very center, where her arms can't reach. She lies on her stomach and talks to me for an hour—soft words, pleading words. I don't understand them, but I understand the exhaustion in her voice. Eventually, she gets the broom —not to hit me, just to guide me out. I hate the broom. I run. She catches me in the hallway. She always catches me.

By the second week, I stop running as far. Not because I've forgiven her. Because running takes energy, and energy is expensive now. I conserve what I have. I pick hiding spots closer to the ground. I let her find me faster.

The foam still comes. Every single time. My body never learns to accept the Oil. But the aftermath gets shorter. I used to drag my face across the rug for twenty minutes. Now it's five. I used to hide until midnight. Now I'm back in my chair by the time the fire burns low.

The Witch notices. She stops crying during the ritual— not because it hurts her less, but because she's run out of tears. Her eyes are red-rimmed and dry. Her hands don't shake as much. We are both learning to survive this.

The house smells different now. Medicine and vinegar. The sharp bite of the Oil, which lingers in the air long after the bottle is closed. The Witch washes her hands constantly—I can smell the soap on her skin, layered over the faint chemical residue that never quite disappears.

There are towels everywhere. On the chair where she holds me. On the floor where I foam. On her lap when she sits, just in case. The cottage has become a hospital. I remember when it smelled like woodsmoke and herbs and us.

Some mornings, I wake up and the burning is quieter. Not gone. Never gone. But the screaming has dropped to a mutter. I can groom my face without flinching. I can sleep without waking every hour to scratch.

On those days, I am the Queen again. I jump on the bed at dawn. I scream at the Witch. *Breakfast! Now!* I sit in the window and chatter at the birds, and my face doesn't hurt when I open my mouth.

The Witch watches me on these days. She doesn't say anything. She just watches, her coffee going cold in her hands, something careful in her expression. She is afraid to believe it. I am afraid too. But I chase the sunbeam anyway.

Jake has learned the rhythm.

He doesn't disappear anymore when the curtains close. He stations himself in the hallway, just outside whatever room the hunt takes place in. Close enough to know what's happening. Far enough to be safe. I don't know why he does this. Maybe he thinks witnessing it is better than imagining it.

He approaches me the same way every time. Slow. Low to the ground. He stops three body-lengths away and waits. If I don't hiss, he comes closer. If I don't growl, he settles behind me.

He grooms my shoulders. My spine. The back of my neck, where the fur is still thick and the skin is still whole. He stops exactly one inch before he reaches the danger zone of my ears. He has learned the map of me—where I end and the sickness begins.

I lean into him. I press my side against his warm orange bulk. I don't say thank you—I am a Cat—but I stop tensing. I let him work. Some nights, we sleep like we used to. A pile of fur on the rug, his chin on my flank, my tail across his paws. Those nights, I almost forget.

The good days come more often. One in a row. Then two. Then three.

The Witch starts humming again while she makes her tea. She stops flinching every time I shake my head. She touches me more—carefully, always carefully—but she touches me. Her fingers find the spots that still feel good. Behind my right ear. Under my chin, on the side that healed.

Then, a victory. It is small. But it is there. The sore on my chin—the one that has been weeping for weeks—is dry.

The Witch notices it first. She touches it with her thumb. I flinch, waiting for the sting. No sting. Just pressure.

"It's healed," she whispers. Her voice cracks. "Missi, it's healed."

I purr. It is a small purr. I remember this feeling—skin that works, fur that lies flat, a body that isn't at war with itself. The Oil is vile. But maybe it is buying me back.

We taper again. The Witch reduces the Sludge.

It happens on the second step of the taper.

I wake up, and I know. It isn't a whisper this time. It is a scream.

The heat is back, but it has moved. It isn't just my left

ear. It isn't just my chin. It is my face, my brow, the skin right above my good eye. It itches. It *itches*. It feels like there are ants crawling under my skin. It feels like a wire is being pulled tight through my skull.

I rub my face against the chair leg. It isn't enough. I rub my face against the carpet. It isn't enough.

The itch screams. *Scratch me. Scratch me or I will drive you mad.*

I can't help it. My back leg comes up. My claws slide out. I aim for the brow. I scratch.

Relief.

For one second, it feels amazing. Then my paw slips.

My claw goes too low. It catches the eyelid. It catches something soft underneath—something that yields, something that shouldn't. A wet, quiet tearing.

Then the agony floods my skull. I can't see. I can't think. Just white, then throbbing red behind my eyelid. I yowl—a sharp, high sound of panic. I squeeze the eye shut. It is wet. It is burning.

And it's not just the eye.

I try to stand. *Ouch.* I lift my paw. I shake it. I try the other paw. *Ouch.*

The black skin of my paw pads is cracking. Peeling. They look like overripe berries splitting their skins. This is new. Before, the fire lived on my face. Now it is in my feet. It has learned to walk.

I limp. I hobble three steps, then I sit down. It hurts to stand.

The Witch puts the Good Food in front of me. Tuna. Shrimp.

I look at it with my one good eye. The other is swollen shut, weeping thick, cloudy tears. The smell of the fish makes my stomach turn.

"Missi, please," she begs. She is crying again. She is always crying now. "Just a bite."

I turn my head away. She reaches for me. She wants to stroke my back. I flinch. I pull my body into a tight ball. *Don't touch me.*

Her hand hovers. Her face crumples, the skin around her eyes going tight and wet. She wants to help. She can't help. Her hands hurt me. Her potions hurt me.

I growl. Low in my throat. *Leave me alone.*

I limp away. My feet burn on the floorboards. I find the darkest corner. Behind the woodpile, where the drafts are cold and the shadows are deep.

Jake tries to follow me. He makes a small chirping sound. He wants to groom me. He wants to fix it. I turn on him.

My lip curls back. My bad eye is shut, oozing. My good eye is wide. I snarl. A real, vicious sound.

He stops. He backs away—but not far. He settles just out of reach and watches me with something new in his eyes. Not the old terror. Something quieter. He is learning that my anger is part of the sickness, not part of me.

I don't recognize the sound I just made. I don't recognize myself.

I am alone.

I curl up in the dust. My eye is throbbing. My feet are burning. My skin is eating me. I wait. I don't know for what. I close my one good eye. I breathe. I count the throbs until they become something I can survive.

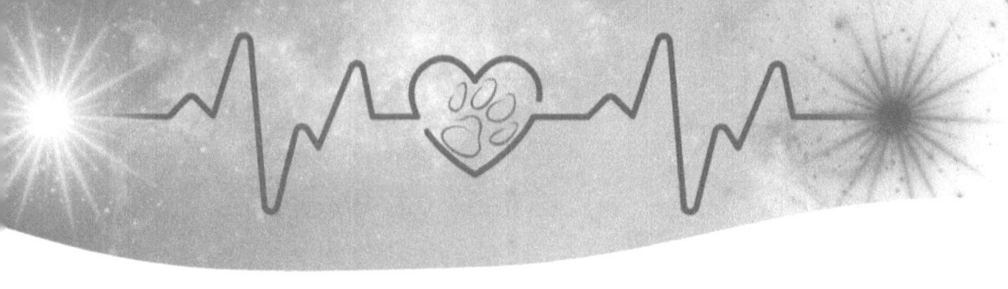

TWELVE

The Specialist

WITCH

I know something is wrong before I find her.

The house is too quiet. No yowling for breakfast. No paws clicking on the floorboards. Jake is sitting by the bedroom door, staring at the gap underneath, making small sounds I've never heard him make before. Not meows. Not chirps. Something lower. Something worried.

"Missi?"

No answer.

I check the chair. Empty. The windowsill. Empty. Under the bed—I get down on my hands and knees, press my cheek to the cold floor, peer into the darkness. Nothing.

The fear starts then. A cold trickle down my spine.

I search the cottage room by room. Behind the sofa. Inside the wardrobe. In the gap between the bookshelf and the wall where she hid during the first flare. Nothing.

"Missi, where are you?"

My voice is too loud. The cottage swallows it.

I find her behind the woodpile. She is a ball of misery in

the dust and the cobwebs, pressed into the darkest corner where the wood meets the stone wall. When I hold up the lantern, she doesn't look up. She doesn't move. She just presses her face harder into her paws.

"Hey," I whisper. "Hey, it's me. What's wrong?"

I reach for her. She flinches—a tiny motion, barely visible, but I feel it in my chest like a punch.

I gently lift her chin. Then I see the eye.

Her right eye—the good eye, the one that healed, the one the Healer said was fine—is clouded over. The surface looks wrong. Melted. Like wax left too close to a flame. In the center, there is a divot, a crater eating into the lens.

"No," I hear myself say. "No, no, no."

I look at her feet. The pads, usually tough and black, are swollen and purple. They look like overripe berries splitting their skins. One of them has cracked open, leaving a bloody print on the wood where she walked.

"Oh, Missi." My voice breaks. "Oh, no."

She doesn't respond. She doesn't lift her head. She doesn't make a sound. She is just... waiting.

The lantern slips from my fingers. It hits the floor with a clatter, the flame guttering but not dying, throwing wild shadows across the walls. I don't pick it up. I sit back on my heels. The dust settles around me.

We did everything right. The doses. The schedule. The hope. None of it mattered.

I don't let myself think. If I think, I'll freeze.

I grab the thick wool blanket from the bed—the one I've been using since I sold my winter cloak. I wrap Missi in it, careful of her feet, careful of the eye she won't open. She is limp in my arms. She weighs nothing and everything.

The carrier is too slow. Too formal. This is not a visit. I run into the rain.

The Healer meets us at the door.

It's past her normal hours—the sign on the door says CLOSED—but she must have seen me coming through the window. She takes one look at the bundle in my arms, at my face, and she waves me straight to the back without a word.

She puts Missi on the metal table. The examination room is cold, and Missi shivers under the blanket. I keep my hand on her side, feeling her ribs expand and contract. Still breathing. Still here.

The Healer unwraps the blanket. She sees the feet first. "When did this start?"

"I don't know. I found her like this. Maybe overnight. Maybe longer." My voice comes out wrong. Too high. Too thin. "I should have checked on her. I should have—"

"Stop." The Healer's voice is firm but not unkind. "You're here now. Let me look."

She examines the paws one by one, turning them gently in her hands. Missi doesn't pull away. She doesn't have the energy. Then the Healer reaches for the light.

"I need to see the eye."

She clicks it on. A bright, focused beam, aimed directly at Missi's face.

Missi screams.

It is a sound I have never heard before. Not the angry

yowl of the medicine ritual. Not the frightened hiss of the carrier. This is something torn from her throat—high and ragged and endless, the sound scraping against the walls of the small room until I want to cover my ears.

The Healer clicks the light off instantly. Her face goes pale.

The room is silent except for Missi's ragged breathing and the rain hammering the roof.

"Corneal melting," the Healer says finally. Her voice is tight, controlled—the voice of someone delivering news they don't want to give. "It's a deep ulcer. Much worse than the first one. The Unbinding isn't just attacking her skin anymore. It's turning on deeper tissue. The bond magic that should be protecting her—it's consuming her instead."

"And the feet?"

"Plasma Cell Pododermatitis. 'Pillow Foot.' The same misfiring. Her body is attacking the fat pads of her paws."

I look at Missi. She is trembling on the table, her bad eye squeezed shut, her swollen feet tucked under her body. She looks half the size she used to be.

"What do we do?" I ask. "We go back to the full dose? We add something new?"

The Healer doesn't answer immediately. She sets her tools down. She leans against the metal counter, shoulders dropping, and presses her palms flat against the surface like she needs the support.

"I am out of options," she says. "I'm sorry."

The words land like a physical blow. The room tilts. I grab the edge of the table to stay upright.

"What do you mean?" I step forward. "You have the

potions. You have the Oil. There must be something else to try—"

"The standard protocols have failed." She turns to face me. "The steroid failed on its own. The Oil isn't holding the line, even at full strength. The suppressants I'm licensed to carry—they're not strong enough for this. If we keep guessing, she is going to lose that eye. Maybe both. Maybe worse."

"So what do we do?" The room feels smaller. The walls feel closer. "Is this… is this the end?"

"No." The Healer's voice softens. "But I can't fix this. Not here. Not with what I have. You need the High Specialists."

She pulls a heavy book from her shelf—a directory of some kind, the pages yellowed and dog-eared from use. She writes two names on a piece of parchment, her handwriting quick and sharp.

"This one," she points to the first name, "is a Dermatologist. A skin mage. They have access to Capital-grade suppressants. Stronger. More targeted."

She points to the second name.

"And this one… this is the Ophthalmologist. The Eye Wizard. He's the best in the kingdom for corneal damage. If anyone can save that eye, it's him."

She looks me dead in the face.

"You need to go there. Not next week. Not in a few days. Now. Tonight, if you can manage it. If we don't treat that melting ulcer aggressively, the eye will rupture. And if the eye ruptures, the infection goes straight to the brain. We would have to—"

She stops herself. She doesn't finish.

I take the paper. It shakes in my hand.

"Specialists," I whisper. "In the Capital?"

"Yes. They're the best. But..." She hesitates. "I have to warn you. It will be significant."

"Significant travel?"

"Significant cost."

Twelve silver. I have twelve silver in the tin at home.

I look at Missi. She is still shivering on the table, wrapped in the blanket that smells like our home. Her paws are swollen. Her eye is melting. She is broken in ways I don't fully understand.

I think of the ledger. I think of the lines I've already crossed out—food, heat, everything that isn't absolutely essential. I can still feel the draft where my good winter cloak used to be. The emergency fund is gone. The backup fund is gone. I've been eating rice and foraged greens for a month.

None of it matters.

"Okay," I say. "Give me the referral."

I move on autopilot. I am not a person anymore. I am a logistics machine, and if I stop to feel anything, the machine will break down.

Travel bag. I grab the canvas satchel from the hook by the door. *Warm blanket.* The wool one is already wrapped around Missi. I take the thin cotton one for myself. I probably won't sleep anyway. *Water bottle.* I fill it at the pump, my hands shaking so badly that water splashes onto my shoes. *The ledger.* I don't know why I pack this. Maybe because I need to believe there will be a future where the numbers matter again.

The carrier. I pull it from the closet. Missi hates this thing—she yowls every time she sees it, fights me every time I try to put her inside. But I can't hold her in a blanket for six hours on a coach. She needs to be contained. Safe.

I line the bottom with the wool blanket, the one that smells like home. I tuck her inside, and she doesn't fight me. She doesn't make a sound. She just curls into the corner and closes her eyes.

That scares me more than the fighting ever did. The fighting, at least, was resistance. This silence feels like surrender—like the bond itself has gone quiet.

I count the money in the tin. Twelve silver. I count it again, as if the number might change. The coach ticket is five. The consultation fee will be at least ten—probably more, for specialists. The medicine... I don't even want to guess.

It isn't enough. It isn't close to enough.

I go to the closet. I pull down the box I haven't opened in years, the one I keep on the highest shelf, behind the spare blankets and the broken lantern I keep meaning to fix. Inside, wrapped in faded velvet, is my mother's locket.

I hold it in my palm. The gold is warm from being stored near the chimney. The chain is delicate—she always said it was too fine for everyday wear, that she was saving it for special occasions. She wore it on my parents' wedding day. She wore it the day I was born. She wore it the last time I saw her, when she pressed it into my hands and told me to keep it safe.

My thumb finds the clasp. I press it. The locket opens.

Inside, a single lock of hair—dark brown, going gray at the edges—is wound around a tiny sprig of dried lavender. Her favorite. The smell has long since faded, but I remember it. I remember her hands in the garden, the purple flowers, the way she hummed while she worked.

I close the locket. The clasp clicks shut.

It was supposed to be my dowry, back when dowries mattered. Then it was supposed to be my retirement, my emergency fund, the thing I would sell only when everything else was gone.

Everything else is gone.

I close my fingers around it. The clasp digs into my palm.

"I'm sorry," I whisper to the empty room. To my mother. To the girl I used to be, the one who thought she'd have a different life. "I'm sorry. I have to."

I put it in my pocket.

I go to the kitchen. I fill a bowl for Jake. This is the hardest part.

He is sitting by the door, watching me pack. His tail is tucked tight against his body. His ears are back. He knows the carrier means bad things—even though I'm not using the carrier this time, he can smell the fear on me. He can smell the sickness on Missi, worse than before.

"I have to go, buddy," I tell him. I kneel down on the cold

floor. My knees ache. Everything aches. "I have to take her to the city. To the doctors there."

He bumps his head against my knee. A desperate, confused gesture. He doesn't understand. He just knows something is wrong, and I'm leaving, and his sister is wrapped in a blanket and she won't move.

"Bessa is coming to feed you," I say. "Twice a day. She'll check your water. She'll make sure you're okay."

He chirps. A small, lost sound. *Where is she? Where are you going? Why does everything smell like blood?*

"I'm going to fix her," I say. "I promise. I'm going to bring her home."

I don't know if I'm lying. I don't know if I can keep this promise.

I kiss the top of his head. His fur is soft against my lips. He smells like dust and home and the life we used to have.

I stand. I pick up Missi's carrier.

Jake moves. He plants himself in front of the door. Not hissing, not aggressive—just there. His orange bulk fills the gap between me and the exit. His eyes are huge and pleading. *Don't go. Don't take her. Don't leave me alone.*

My throat closes.

"I have to, buddy." My voice is barely a whisper. "I have to."

He doesn't move. I have to step around him, my hip brushing his side, feeling him press against my leg as I pass. I don't look back. If I look back, I won't leave.

Behind me, I hear him chirp once more. Then silence.

I walk out into the rain.

The Pawnbroker's shop is on the way to the coach station.

The bell above the door jingles when I push it open. The sound is absurdly cheerful. Inside, the shop smells of dust and old metal and other people's desperation.

The man behind the counter is thin, with spectacles perched on his nose and ink stains on his fingers. He doesn't smile when he sees me. He doesn't frown. His face is perfectly neutral—the face of someone who has seen a thousand people walk through that door clutching the last thing they own.

I don't haggle. I don't have time.

I set the locket on the counter. The gold catches the lamplight, and for a moment it looks like something precious. Something that matters.

He picks it up. He weighs it on a small brass scale. He examines it with a jeweler's loupe, turning it this way and that. He doesn't look at me when he speaks.

"Thirty silver."

He pushes the coins across the counter with one finger. It's worth fifty. Maybe more. My mother would have said sixty.

"Done," I say.

He counts out the coins. I watch his fingers move— quick, practiced, indifferent. To him, this is just another transaction. Another desperate person trading memories for metal.

I snatch the coins up. I shove them into my pocket without counting them again.

I leave my mother's memory on his counter, and I run. The coins are cold and heavy against my leg, a terrible weight where the locket used to be.

The coach station is chaos.

People shouting. Horses stamping. The smell of wet wool and manure and coal smoke. I push through the crowd, Missi clutched against my chest, until I find the ticket window.

"One to the Capital," I say. "The next coach."

The clerk looks at the bundle in my arms. "Is that a cat?"

"She's sick. She's seeing a specialist."

"Pets are extra."

"How much extra?"

"Two silver."

I close my eyes. Seven silver for the ticket instead of five. That leaves me thirty-five for the specialists. It won't be enough. I pay anyway.

The coach ride is six hours of hell.

The carriage is crowded. A merchant in a fur-trimmed

coat, taking up more than his share of the bench. A farmer with a crate of chickens that cluck and shift with every bump. A young couple pressed close together, whispering to each other, lost in their own small happiness.

I sit in the corner, as far from the others as I can get. The carrier is on my lap, my arms wrapped around it. Through the mesh door, I can see Missi curled in the back corner, pressed against the blanket. She hasn't moved since I put her inside. She hasn't made a sound.

The carriage sways and bumps over the cobblestones. Every jolt goes through my arms, through the carrier, into her body. I try to hold it steady, try to absorb the shock, but the road is bad and the springs are worse.

The merchant wrinkles his nose. "What's that smell?"

"Medicine," I say. My voice comes out flat. Hard. "She's sick."

"Is it contagious?"

"No."

He doesn't look convinced. He shifts as far away from me as the cramped space allows. I don't care. I don't have room to care about anything except the small body in the carrier.

Every ten minutes, I open the mesh door just enough to slip my hand inside and check her breathing. It is shallow. Fast. Her heart flutters against my palm like a trapped bird. *Still alive,* I tell myself. *Still alive. Still alive.*

The countryside rolls by outside the window. Gray fields. Gray sky. Gray rain streaking the glass like tears. The world looks like I feel—washed out, colorless, barely holding together.

I think about the eye. *Melting.* The word keeps echoing

in my head. What does that even mean? What does it look like when an eye melts? I think about the paws. *Bursting.* The image of those swollen, purple pads. The bloody print on the wood. I think about the money in my pocket. Thirty-five silver after the ticket. The Oil alone cost forty. What do specialists charge? Fifty? A hundred? More?

Missi shifts inside the carrier. A small, pained whimper escapes her—the first sound she's made in hours.

The sound cuts through everything else.

I will beg. If I have to, I will get on my knees in that expensive stone building and I will beg. I will scrub their floors. I will wash their windows. I will sell every piece of clothing I own except what I'm wearing. I will do whatever it takes.

"I know," I whisper through the mesh. "I know it hurts. We're almost there. Just hold on. Just a little longer."

I don't know if she can hear me. I don't know if it matters. I say it anyway. I say it for both of us.

The Capital is overwhelming.

The coach pulls through the city gates just as the rain stops, and for a moment the clouds break and weak sunlight streams down onto streets that are wider than any I've ever seen.

Everything is loud. Cart wheels on cobblestones. Street vendors shouting. A thousand conversations in a dozen languages, blending into a roar of noise that makes my head pound. Everything is tall. The buildings loom four, five, six stories high, blocking out the sky. Towers and spires and chimneys belching smoke. Signs hanging from every doorway, painted with symbols I don't recognize. Everything smells wrong. Coal smoke and sewage and too many people packed too close together. No woodsmoke. No herbs. No clean rain on green fields.

I step off the coach and nearly get knocked over by a man rushing past with a stack of boxes. No one apologizes. No one even looks at me.

I clutch Missi against my chest and navigate the streets using the Healer's map. Left at the fountain with the stone fish. Right at the tavern with the red door. Straight until you see the ironwork gates.

The Institute of Ocular Magic.

The building isn't a cottage. It isn't even a house. It is a stone fortress, four stories tall, with columns flanking the entrance and windows that gleam with expensive glass. A sign hangs above the door, the letters picked out in gold leaf:

THE INSTITUTE OF OCULAR MAGIC

Specialists in Diseases of the EyeBy Appointment Only

I stop at the bottom of the steps. My feet don't want to move. This place wasn't built for people like me. It was built for the wealthy, the connected, the ones who never had to choose between medicine and food.

The carrier shifts in my arms. Missi whimpers again.

I force my feet up the steps.

I look down at myself. My boots are caked with mud from the run through the rain. My cloak—not my good cloak, the thin one I kept—is patched and faded and damp at the hem. The carrier in my arms is battered, the plastic scuffed, the blanket inside stained with something dark. Blood, maybe. Medicine. The residue of catastrophe.

I look like exactly what I am: a poor village witch who is in way over her head.

I take a breath. I square my shoulders.

My hand goes to my pocket. The coins are there—thirty-five silver, cold and heavy, bought with my mother's memory.

I am not a poor village witch right now. Right now, I am her guardian. I am the only thing standing between her and the dark. I have thirty-five silver and a dying cat.

I push the heavy oak door open.

The lobby is everything I expected. High ceilings. Polished marble floors. A chandelier dripping with crystals that catch the light and scatter it into rainbows. There are plush chairs along the walls, occupied by well-dressed witches and wizards with familiars in expensive carriers— gilded things with velvet linings and polished brass latches. A parrot in a gilded cage. A small dog with a ribbon in its fur. A cat—sleek, well-groomed, nothing like the miserable creature huddled in my battered plastic box.

The air smells of jasmine and money. The kind of perfume that costs more than my monthly wage.

They all look at me. They all look away.

The receptionist is a young woman in a pristine white robe. Her hair is perfect. Her nails are perfect. She looks at me with the polite, distant expression of someone who has already decided I don't belong here.

"Can I help you?" she asks.

I walk up to the counter. I set the carrier down on the polished wood—gently, so gently, even though the receptionist flinches at the scuffed plastic touching her clean surface.

"Help us," I say. My voice doesn't shake. I won't let it shake. "Please."

The receptionist opens her mouth—to tell me I need an appointment, probably, or that the consultation fee is due upfront, or that perhaps I should try the charity clinic on the other side of town.

She sees a beggar. Fine. Let her see a disaster instead.

I don't let her speak.

"Her eye is melting," I say. "The Healer in Miren Hollow sent us. She said you're the only ones who can save it. She said if we don't act now, it will rupture."

The receptionist hesitates. She looks at the carrier on her counter. She looks at my face.

Something in her expression shifts.

"Wait here," she says. "I'll get the doctor."

THIRTEEN

The Wizards

MISSI

The new place smells like fear.

Not the earthy, herbal fear of the Village Healer's office. This is different. This place smells sharp—like lightning trapped in a bottle. Like bleach and cold metal and the terror of a thousand other animals who came here before me.

The carrier sits on a hard chair. I am curled in the back corner, pressed against the plastic wall, making myself as small as possible. The carrier smells like home—like the blanket the Witch tucked around me, like woodsmoke and herbs—but outside the carrier, everything is wrong.

It is cold here. The kind of cold that seeps through fur, through skin, into bone. I am already shivering, and we haven't even started.

The Witch sits beside me. I can see her through the mesh door—her hands clasped in her lap, her knee bouncing. She smells like rain and sweat and fear. Her fear is almost as strong as mine.

The waiting room is large. Larger than any room I've ever been in. The ceiling is high and distant. The floor is polished stone that echoes when people walk across it. There are other animals here—I can hear them, smell them, sense their misery. A dog whimpers somewhere to my left. Low, mournful. *I don't want to be here. I don't want to be here.* A bird rustles in a covered cage. The fabric muffles its panic, but I can hear the frantic flutter of wings against bars. Another cat—I catch the scent through the mesh—is silent. That silence is worse than any sound. That is the silence of a creature who has stopped fighting.

I wonder if that's what I will become. A quiet thing in a box, waiting for strangers to decide my fate.

No. I still have claws. I still have teeth. I am not silent yet.

I press myself harder into the corner. I close my eyes. I pretend I am somewhere else.

"Missi?"

The Witch's voice. A hand on the carrier. We are moving.

I open my eyes. We are leaving the waiting room, following a woman in a white coat down a long hallway. The floor is cold even through the plastic bottom of the carrier. The lights are bright—too bright—buzzing faintly overhead.

The room they take us to is small and white and smells like nothing. That is almost worse than the fear smell.

Nothing is not natural. Nothing means chemicals so strong they have erased every trace of life.

The carrier opens. I don't come out.

"Come on, Missi," the Witch says. Her hand reaches in. She smells like home, but her fingers are trembling. "It's okay. I'm right here."

She lifts me out. I feel her shaking. I look at this white room, this steel table, this place that smells of erasure. Fighting here would cost me. I decide to save it.

I go limp in her arms—not relaxed, just waiting. Conserving.

She places me on a table. It is cold. It is slippery stainless steel. I try to dig my claws in, but my paws are swollen and the surface is too smooth. I slide. I crouch low, pressing my belly to the metal, making myself a puddle of misery.

A stranger enters. He is tall. He wears white robes that rustle when he moves. His hands are gloved—I can smell the rubber, the faint chemical tang of whatever coats them. He smells like nothing. Just like the room. He has scrubbed himself clean of any scent that might tell me who he is, what he wants, whether he is safe.

In my world, a creature with no scent is wrong. It means the tracks have been erased. It means something is hunting, and it doesn't want you to know until it's too late.

He is not safe. I know this in my bones.

"The Eye Wizard," the Witch calls him. Her voice is small.

He doesn't greet me. He doesn't offer a hand to sniff. He just reaches for my face.

I growl. Low. A warning that comes from deep in my chest. *My face is fire. Do not touch the fire.*

His eyes flick to mine. Cold. Assessing. The look of something deciding whether I am worth the trouble. He reaches anyway.

The exam starts normal. He looks at my ears. He looks at my teeth. He listens to my chest with a cold metal disc that makes me flinch. The Witch holds me steady, her hands warm on my shoulders, her voice murmuring things I don't understand.

Then he reaches for a small bottle.

"I need to examine the damaged eye," he says. "This will help me see inside."

He tips my head back. He pries my eyelid open—the bad eye, the one that won't stop weeping. A drop falls onto my eyeball. It stings. A sharp, chemical bite that makes me jerk. The Witch tightens her grip.

"Hold her steady," the Wizard says.

The lights go out.

Darkness crashes down. My body goes rigid. This is wrong—darkness means hiding, means safety, but this darkness is a trap. I can feel him moving in it, circling, and I cannot see where he is. I can barely see the Witch's outline. I can barely see the Wizard moving in the shadows.

Then comes the light.

Not the overhead lights. A different light. A small, focused beam that cuts through the darkness like a blade. He aims it at my eye. At my damaged, weeping, burning eye.

The light hits the wound.

Fire.

It doesn't pierce—it *floods.* Every nerve in my eye screams at once. The damaged tissue, raw and exposed, recoils from the brightness. I can't see. I can't think. There is only the light and the agony and the desperate need to make it stop.

I twist my head. I open my mouth. I bite.

My teeth find his hand—the gloved fingers holding my eyelid open. I clamp down hard, feeling the rubber compress, feeling something solid underneath. He yanks his hand back.

The light disappears. The room is dark again.

"Missi!" The Witch's voice is sharp with panic. "No!"

I am panting. My heart is racing. I can taste rubber and chemicals on my tongue.

The Wizard steps back. He is flexing his hand, checking his fingers. I didn't break the skin—the glove was thick—but I felt his flesh between my teeth. I wanted to hurt him. I wanted to make him stop.

His eyes find me in the dark. The cold assessment is gone. Now there is something harder. Something that has decided I am a problem.

"Feisty," he says. His voice is calm. Almost amused.

Feisty. As if this is a game. As if the fire in my eye is entertainment.

I am not feisty. I am in agony. But he doesn't understand the difference. He doesn't care to.

"Hold her head," he says to the Witch. "Firmly this time."

The Witch leans over me. Her hands grip my skull, pressing me down into the cold steel. I feel her chest against my back. I feel her shaking. And I feel something else. Something wrong in the space between us—the place where the bond lives, the warm thread that connects us. It feels stretched. Strained. Like something pulling too tight.

She is helping him. She is holding me down for the creature who hurts me.

"I'm sorry, Missi," she whispers. "I'm sorry. Just a little more."

The light comes back.

I scream.

It is not a yowl. It is not a hiss. It is a raw, throat-tearing sound of pure protest. I thrash against the Witch's hands, but she holds me down. I try to turn my head, but she pins me in place. The Wizard leans closer. He studies the ruin of my eye while I scream and scream and scream.

It lasts forever. It lasts a few seconds.

The light clicks off.

"Deep ulceration," he says. His voice is clinical. Bored. "But the globe is intact. We caught it in time."

I am trembling so hard my teeth chatter. The Witch's hands relax on my head, but she doesn't let go. Something shifts in her scent. The sharp edge of terror dulls, replaced by something heavier. Grim. Determined. She understood something in those words. I don't know what.

She is crying. I can smell the salt.

The Wizard talks to the Witch.

I don't understand the words. I am too tired, too wrung out, too focused on the throbbing in my eye. But I catch fragments.

"...antiviral drops, twice a day..."

"...serum, four times a day..."

"...ointment for lubrication and infection prevention, three to four times..."

"...pain management... every eight to twelve hours... mix it with food..."

The Witch is nodding. She is writing things down. Her hands are still shaking. The Wizard hands her a bag. It clinks with bottles. More medicine. More torture. I can smell the chemicals through the paper.

He also hands her a small packet.

"Cleaning cloths," he says. "The discharge will be significant for the first few days. Keep the area clean. Wipe gently. Don't let it crust over."

The Witch takes everything. She thanks him.

She *thanks* him.

The creature who held me down and burned my eye with light, and she bows her head and offers gratitude like he is pack. Like he belongs to us. I don't understand. I will never understand.

She puts me back in the carrier. I collapse onto the blanket, exhausted, my eye burning, my body shaking.

We leave the cold room. We walk back down the long hallway. We pass through the waiting room with its whimpering dogs and silent cats. I brace for the outside. For the smell of rain and horses and the carriage that will take us home.

We do not go home.

The second place is smaller. Warmer. But it still smells like fear.

The Witch carries me inside. I am too tired to look around. I just curl in the carrier and wait for whatever comes next. Another stranger. Another exam room. Another cold table.

The Skin Mage.

She smells different from the Eye Wizard—less like nothing, more like sulfur and something sharp and green. Mint, maybe. She moves differently too. Slower. Gentler. She actually looks at me before she touches me.

"Hello, little one," she says. Her voice is soft. "Let's see what we're dealing with."

She looks at my paws. She turns them over in her hands, examining the swollen pads, the cracked skin. Even her careful touch makes me flinch. The pads feel like they might burst at any moment.

She pauses. Her fingers hover over my left front paw—the worst one.

"This one is hotter than the others," she murmurs. "The inflammation is concentrated here. Has she been favoring it?"

The Witch nods. "She limps on that side."

The Mage makes a note. Something in her eyes sharpens —not cruel, just focused. Her gentleness is a tool. She is reading me.

She looks at my face. The sores. The patches where the fur has fallen out. The raw, red edges where my skin is attacking itself.

"Classic presentation," she murmurs. Not to me. To the Witch. "The steroids aren't holding it."

The Witch makes a small sound. Agreement. Defeat.

"The current medications," the Mage says, "they're hard on the body. The steroid especially. How long has she been on the full dose?"

"Weeks," the Witch says. "We tried to taper. It came back worse."

"Her blood work shows elevated glucose. She's trending toward diabetic range." The Mage's voice is serious. "If we keep her on high-dose steroids much longer, we risk pushing her over that edge. Diabetes is manageable, but it's another complication you don't want."

I don't understand the words. But I understand the Witch's scent changing—a new note rising through the fear. Something colder. Something that smells like the future closing in.

"There's another option," the Mage says. "A different class of immunosuppressant. It's not a steroid—it works differently. It's typically used for…" She pauses. "For very sick patients. Patients undergoing aggressive treatments for other conditions."

"Will it work?"

"It should. It targets the immune response without the metabolic side effects of steroids. No glucose spikes. No increased thirst or hunger." She looks at me. "It will take time to build up in her system. Two weeks, maybe three. We keep her on a low dose of the steroid to bridge the gap, then taper off entirely once the new medication takes over."

More medicine. More weeks. More poison. But the Witch is nodding. The Witch is agreeing. The Witch is willing to try.

The Mage takes something from me—a small scrape of skin, a tuft of fur. I don't growl. I don't flinch. I remember the sound I made at the Eye Wizard. The warning that came from deep in my chest. I have no warning left. I have spent it all. I barely feel the scrape. I am beyond feeling.

She hands the Witch another bag. More bottles. More instructions.

Then, finally, we leave.

The ride home is long.

I am curled in the carrier, pressed into the corner, my eye throbbing under the drops they put in it. My paws ache. My whole body aches. The Witch talks to me through the mesh. Soft words. I don't listen. I am too tired to listen.

The carriage sways. The world passes by outside—I can see fragments of it through the mesh, gray and blurred and meaningless. I am quiet. I don't have the energy to cry. I don't have the energy to fight. I just exist, small and broken, in the corner of my plastic box.

Time passes. I drift.

In the darkness behind my eyes, I smell bleach. I smell cold metal. I feel the light burning into my skull.

Then—something else. A smell that cuts through the memory like a blade.

Woodsmoke. Herbs. The particular mustiness of old books. The lingering trace of orange fur.

Home.

I lift my head.

The smells grow stronger as the carriage slows. I recognize the rattle of the wheels on the cobblestones near our lane. I recognize the creak of the turn by the old well. We are close. We are almost there.

The first yowl comes out before I can stop it.

It is the first sound I have *wanted* to make all day. Not a scream forced out by pain. Not a growl of warning. This is mine. This is need. Low, at first. Then louder. A demand. A plea.

Home. I can smell home. Let me out. Take me home.

The Witch makes a sound that might be a laugh or might be a sob.

"Almost there, Missi. Almost there."

I yowl again. And again. The sound tears at my raw throat, but I can't stop.

Home. Home. Home.

The carriage stops. The door opens. The Witch lifts my carrier. Cold air. The smell of rain. The smell of our garden, our door, our life.

She carries me inside.

Jake is there. He is sitting in the middle of the room, exactly where he was sitting when we left. His eyes are huge. His tail is tucked. He looks at the carrier like he's afraid of what he'll find inside. Then he takes a step forward. And another. His ears are flat, his body low, but he is moving toward me despite his fear.

The Witch sets the carrier down. She opens the door.

I don't bolt out. I don't have the strength to bolt. I walk out. Slowly. My paws hurt on the floorboards. My eye weeps under its shield.

Jake approaches. Cautious. He sniffs my face. He smells the chemicals, the strangers, the fear. He makes a small sound. A chirp. *You're back.*

I press my forehead against his.

I am back. I am broken and exhausted and full of new poisons. But I am back.

The Witch sits down on the floor beside us. She doesn't reach for me. She just sits there, close, letting me know she's here.

All day, hands have grabbed me. Held me down. Forced things into my eye. The Wizard. The Mage. Even the Witch herself, pinning my skull to the table. Now she sits. She waits. She lets me choose.

It is the first correct thing a human has done all day.

I lie down on the rug. Jake lies down next to me.

I close my eyes.

The Long Watch

WITCH

The first night home, I don't sleep.

I sit at the kitchen table with the paper bag from the specialists spread out in front of me. Bottles and vials and tubes, each with its own label, its own schedule, its own set of instructions. I have notes from both appointments—the Eye Wizard's cramped handwriting, the Skin Mage's neat printed list—and I am trying to make sense of them.

The clock on the mantle ticks. It is 8:00 PM. Missi is behind the wood stove, where she retreated the moment I let her out of the carrier. Jake is sitting in the middle of the room, looking back and forth between her hiding spot and me, confused by everything.

I make a chart.

I use the back of an old receipt, the only blank paper I can find. I draw lines. I write times.

8:00 AM — Pain medication. Serum drops.

9:00 AM — Ointment.
10:00 AM — Antibiotic drops.
12:00 PM — Serum drops.
1:00 PM — Ointment.
4:00 PM — Serum drops.
5:00 PM — Ointment.
8:00 PM — Serum drops. Pain medication.
9:00 PM — Ointment.
10:00 PM — Antibiotic drops.

Plus the new suppressant from the Skin Mage—the one that replaces the steroid and the Oil. Once a day, mixed into food. Plus cleaning the discharge from around her eye. The Wizard said it would be significant for the first few days. He gave me special cloths, soft and damp, that won't irritate the damaged tissue.

I count the doses. Ten separate times I have to catch her, hold her, put something in or on her eye. Ten times a day she has to endure me.

I stare at the chart. It looks like a battle plan. It feels like a prison sentence.

The clock ticks. 8:15 PM. I have forty-five minutes until the ointment. Then an hour until the antibiotic. Then I can sleep—if sleep will come.

I put my head down on the table. Just for a moment. Just to rest my eyes.

I jerk awake to the sound of the clock striking ten.

The chart is stuck to my cheek. I peel it off, blinking in the candlelight. 10:00 PM. Antibiotic. I missed the 9:00 ointment.

My hands go cold. I scramble for the bottles, knocking the serum vial sideways. How long was I asleep? An hour? The ointment was supposed to be at 9:00. The eye needs the lubrication. What if the shield dried out? What if—

I force myself to breathe. One missed dose. One. The Wizard said consistency matters, but he also said the shield protects the cornea. One missed ointment won't undo everything.

I grab both bottles—the ointment and the antibiotic. I'll do them together. Close enough.

I go to the wood stove.

"Missi?"

No answer. I can see her shadow in the gap, pressed against the wall.

"I have to do your eye, sweetheart. I'm sorry."

I reach in. She doesn't fight me, but she doesn't help either. She goes limp, a dead weight, and I have to drag her out by the scruff.

Her eye looks terrible in the candlelight. The shield the Wizard put on is still there—a clear disc that covers the damaged cornea—but around the edges, thick yellowish discharge has crusted. I reach for the cleaning cloth. She flinches when I touch her face. A full-body shudder.

"I know," I whisper. "I know it hurts. I'll be gentle."

I wipe away the crust. Gently. Slowly. The cloth comes away yellow and sticky. Underneath, the skin is red and inflamed. Then the ointment. I pull her lower lid down, squeeze a ribbon of the thick gel along the pink tissue. She squeezes her eye shut immediately, and the ointment spreads, clouding her vision. Then I squeeze a single drop of the antibiotic into the eye.

"Done," I say. "You're done for tonight. You can go."

She doesn't go immediately. She sits there, blinking, disoriented by the blur of the ointment. After a moment, she turns and limps back to the wood stove.

I sit on the floor. I look at the clock. Ten hours until the next dose. 8:00 AM. Pain medication and serum. Ten hours seems like a lifetime. Ten hours seems like nothing.

I should sleep. I should try to sleep. Tomorrow the schedule starts again—ten doses spread across fourteen hours, almost one every hour, no break longer than three hours.

I pull a blanket off the chair. I lie down on the floor, close enough to the wood stove that I could reach her if I needed to, far enough that she doesn't feel crowded. Jake comes over. He sniffs my face, then settles against my legs.

I close my eyes. The clock ticks.

The alarm goes off at 8:00 AM.

I wake in the gray morning light, groggy and disoriented. For a moment I don't know where I am. Then I feel the hard floor under my hip, the cold draft from the door, and I remember.

Pain medication. Serum. 8:00 AM. The day begins.

I fumble for the candle, then realize I don't need it—the sun is up. Pale light filters through the windows. Outside, birds are singing. Inside, my cat is dying. No. Not dying. Healing. Maybe healing.

The bottles are still on the table where I left them. The serum is cold—I've been keeping it in a bowl of water from the well, the closest thing I have to refrigeration. The Wizard said it needs to stay cold or it loses potency.

Missi is still behind the wood stove. She hasn't moved.

I mix the pain medication into a small dish of the soft food she likes—the expensive kind, the kind I can barely afford now. I set it near the gap in the wood stove.

"Breakfast," I say softly. "With your medicine. Please eat."

She doesn't come out. I wait. After a few minutes, I see her nose appear, sniffing. Then her face. She looks at the food. She looks at me. She eats. Slowly, suspiciously, but she eats.

One dose down. Nine to go.

I reach in for the serum drop. She flinches but doesn't run. She's learning that running doesn't help.

9:00 AM. Ointment. 10:00 AM. Antibiotic. The morning blurs into a rhythm of bottles and drops and her small body tensing under my hands. 12:00 PM. Serum. 1:00 PM. Ointment.

I try to eat something between doses. A piece of bread. It tastes like nothing. I chew and swallow mechanically, watching the clock, counting the minutes until the next dose.

4:00 PM. Serum. 5:00 PM. Ointment.

The afternoon light fades. I light the candle. I prepare the evening pain medication, mixing it into another dish of soft food. She eats this one faster—she's learning that the food makes the pain quieter.

8:00 PM. Serum. Pain medication. 9:00 PM. Ointment. 10:00 PM. Antibiotic.

Done. The day is done.

I sit on the floor. I am shaking. Not from cold—from exhaustion, from the effort of holding it together, from the relentless rhythm of catch-hold-drop-release, catch-hold-drop-release, ten times, every single day.

Tomorrow I do it again.

By the third day, I have lost track of time.

The schedule has become my entire world. I wake, I check the clock, I give the drops. I eat something—usually just bread, sometimes nothing—and I check the clock again. I give more drops. I clean the discharge. I apply the ointment. I check the clock.

The chart on the table is covered in check marks. Each one is a dose completed, a battle won. But the battles never stop. There is always another dose, another alarm, another moment of dragging her out from behind the stove and holding her still while she trembles.

I haven't left the cottage since we got home. I can't. The schedule doesn't allow for leaving. The serum has to be given every four hours, the ointment every four, and if I miss a dose—

I can't miss a dose. If I miss a dose, the eye melts again. The Wizard was very clear about that.

So I stay. I sit at the table. I stare at the clock. I wait for the next alarm.

On the fourth day, I open the ledger.

I have been avoiding it. I knew the numbers would be bad. But I can't avoid it forever.

I sit at the table with the candle burning low and I add up the damage.

Coach fare (round trip with pet fee): 14 silver.
Eye Wizard consultation: 25 silver.
Skin Mage consultation: 15 silver.
Medications (eye): 18 silver.
Medications (suppressant): 30 silver.
Boarding house (one night): 2 silver.
Food (Capital): 1 silver.
Total: 105 silver.

I had forty-two silver when I arrived. The locket money plus what was left in the tin.

I stare at the difference. Sixty-three silver. I owe sixty-three silver that I do not have.

The Eye Wizard's office let me pay half upfront and half "upon receipt of invoice." The invoice will come. Probably within the week. And when it does, I will have to find thirty silver I do not have to pay for treatment I have already received.

I look around the cottage. What else is there to sell? The furniture is old and worn. The pots are dented. The blankets are patched. There is nothing left. I have already sold everything that had value.

I close the ledger. I put my head in my hands.

I don't cry. I'm too tired to cry. The tears would take energy I don't have. I just sit there, in the dark, and I breathe.

Jake is struggling.

He doesn't understand what happened. He doesn't understand why his sister hides behind the stove and won't play with him. He doesn't understand why I keep grabbing her and holding her down and making her make those terrible sounds.

He follows me everywhere now. When I sit at the table, he sits at my feet. When I lie on the floor, he presses against my legs. When I go to the wood stove to get Missi, he comes too, hovering at the edge, watching with huge worried eyes.

He has started grooming himself too much. I noticed it on the third day—a bald patch forming on his belly, the fur licked away in anxious circles. He is eating his own stress, swallowing it down, turning it inward.

I should comfort him. I should play with him, reassure him, give him the attention he needs. I don't have the energy. I give him food. I give him water. I scratch behind his ears when he pushes his head into my hand. But I can't give him more than that. I am empty. Everything I have goes into the schedule, the drops, the chart on the table.

He deserves better. They both do.

The burnout creeps up slowly.

At first, I think I'm just tired. Normal tired. The kind of tired you get from not sleeping enough, from waking up every four hours to give medication to a cat who hates you for it.

But by the fifth day, it's more than that.

My hands shake when I try to light the candle. Not a little tremor—a real shake, visible, uncontrollable. I have to grip the match with both hands to keep it steady. I forget to eat. I look at the bread on the counter and I know I should eat it, but the thought of chewing and swallowing feels like too much work. I drink water instead. Water is easier.

I lose words. Simple words. I stand at the table, looking

at the bottles, and I can't remember which one is the serum and which one is the antibiotic. They look the same. I have to read the labels every time, even though I've read them a hundred times before.

I catch myself staring at nothing. I'll be sitting at the table, and I'll realize that ten minutes have passed and I haven't moved. I've just been looking at the wall, my mind completely blank. The clock ticks and I don't hear it.

This is what it feels like to run out. This is what it feels like when there's nothing left to give.

But the schedule doesn't care. The schedule keeps going.

8:00 AM. Serum. Antibiotic. Pain medication.

I get up. I light the candle. I get the bottles. I keep going.

On the sixth day, I see something that might be hope.

I am cleaning the discharge from Missi's eye—the morning routine, soft cloth, gentle pressure—when I notice that there's less of it than yesterday.

I pause. I look closer.

The crust around the edge of the shield is thinner. The yellow color is lighter. The skin underneath, while still red, doesn't look quite as angry.

"Missi," I whisper. "Hold still. Let me see."

She doesn't hold still—she never holds still—but I manage to get a good look before she pulls away.

The eye itself is still cloudy. The shield is still in place.

But something about it looks different. Less like melting wax. More like tissue that might actually heal.

I don't want to hope. Every time I thought we were getting better, something worse happened. But I let myself think, for the first time in days: *maybe.*

I finish the cleaning. I apply the ointment. I let her go.

She limps back to the wood stove, and I sit at the table, and I look at the chart covered in check marks, and I hold onto that word. *Maybe.*

The urge to explain is a constant ache.

I sit on the floor near the wood stove in the evenings, after the last ointment, when the cottage is quiet and dark. I can see her shadow in the gap. I can hear her breathing.

I want to tell her so many things.

I want to say: *I didn't take you to those strangers because I wanted to hurt you. I took you because they were the only ones who could save your eye.*

I want to say: *The drops sting, but the melting stings more. I'm choosing the smaller pain to prevent the larger one.*

I want to say: *I sold my mother's locket for you. The only thing I had left of her. I would do it again. I would do it a hundred times.*

I want to say: *Please don't look at me like I'm the enemy. I'm the only one fighting for you.*

But the familiar bond doesn't work that way.

We share feelings. We share moods. I know when she's

in pain; she knows when I'm afraid. But we don't share logic. We don't share reasons. To her, I am the one who holds her down. I am the one who puts stinging liquid in her eye. I am the one who drags her out of her safe dark hiding spot and makes her endure things she doesn't understand.

She can't know that every drop is an act of love. She can't know that I cry after she limps away. She can't know that I would trade places with her in an instant if I could.

She only knows what she experiences. And her experience is pain.

I carry the knowledge alone. The reasons. The costs. The desperate hope that it's all worth something. It's lonely. It's heavier than I expected anything to be.

But someone has to carry it. And there's no one else.

Night falls on the seventh day.

I do the 10:00 PM antibiotic. Missi endures it with her usual limp resignation. She retreats to the wood stove. I blow out the candle.

I should go to bed. A real bed—I haven't slept in my own bed since we got home. I've been on the floor every night, close to her, close to the stove. But the floor has become familiar now. The bed feels too far away.

I pull the blanket over myself. Jake settles against my legs, already half-asleep. The fire has burned down to embers, casting a faint orange glow across the floorboards.

I set the alarm for 8:00 AM. The serum. Always the serum.

I close my eyes.

I don't know what wakes me.

It's not the alarm—the clock hasn't struck yet. It's not Jake—he's still asleep, snoring softly. It's not a sound from outside.

It's a warmth. A small, slight warmth, pressed against my arm.

I open my eyes, just barely. Just enough to see.

Missi has come out from behind the stove.

She is lying beside me, not on me, but against me. Her back is pressed to my forearm. Her head is tucked under her tail. She is curled into a tight ball, shivering slightly, her bandaged paw tucked against her chest.

She isn't asking for pets. She isn't purring. She isn't even looking at me. She is just here. For warmth, probably. Or maybe to check that I haven't left her again.

I don't move. I don't reach for her. I barely breathe.

I know what this is. This is not forgiveness. This is not trust rebuilt. This is just a cat who is cold and tired and has decided that the warm body on the floor is marginally better than the cold gap behind the stove.

But it's something.

After a week of flinching. After a week of hiding. After a week of looking at me with that flat, betrayed stare. She is here. She is touching me. She chose to come closer instead of staying away.

I lie perfectly still. I let myself be furniture. I let myself be a heat source. I let her take whatever she needs without asking for anything in return.

The fire crackles. Jake snores. The clock ticks toward the next alarm. We lie there in the dark, the three of us. Broken things, all of us. Propping each other up.

Then the alarm goes off.

Click-click-click.

Missi goes rigid against my arm. She knows what that sound means. She pulls away. She looks at me with her one good eye, the pupil wide in the darkness.

I reach for the bottle on the table. My hand moves slowly. I don't want to startle her.

"I'm sorry," I whisper. "I have to. But I'll be quick. I promise."

She doesn't run. She doesn't hide.

She sits there, watching me, waiting for the drop.

It's not much. It's not forgiveness. It's not trust.

But it's a start.

FIFTEEN

Maybe

MISSI

The morning starts with a flinch.

It is a reflex. I wake up on the floor beside the Witch, the gray light of dawn filtering through the curtains, and my body tightens in anticipation. I am waiting for the scream. I am waiting for the fire in my face, the throbbing in my feet, the sharp needle-stab in my eye.

I lie perfectly still. I hold my breath. I wait.

... Nothing.

Well, not nothing. My eye feels heavy, weighed down by the plastic shield the Wizard glued to it. My feet feel stiff, the skin tight and dry. My mouth tastes like the remnants of last night's poison.

But the fire is gone.

The screaming heat that has lived under my skin for weeks, the noise that drowned out every other thought, has quieted to a low, distant hum.

I blink. The plastic lens slides over my eye. It is annoying

—like a piece of grit I can't wash away—but it doesn't hurt. The sharp, stabbing agony of the ulcer is muffled.

I slowly uncurl my legs. I stretch one front paw. Then the other. My pads touch the floorboards. I brace for the burn.

It is just pressure. Just wood against skin.

I sit up. I am suspicious. The burning has tricked me before. It has retreated only to ambush me the moment I let my guard down. I am not a fool. I will not celebrate.

But I will walk to the kitchen.

The Witch is already awake.

She is sitting at the table, her hands wrapped around a mug of tea that went cold an hour ago. She is staring at the wall. She looks older than she did before the Capital. There are dark circles under her eyes, and her shoulders are hunched, as if she is waiting for a blow.

She hears my claws on the wood. She freezes. She doesn't turn around immediately. I can smell her fear— acrid and sharp. She is afraid to look at me. She is afraid I will be bleeding again.

I walk into her line of sight. I don't limp. I don't crouch. I walk with my tail at a careful forty-five-degree angle.

She looks down. Her eyes go to my feet. Then my face. She lets out a breath that sounds like a collapsing lung.

"Morning, Missi," she whispers.

I look at her. *Morning.*

Usually, this is the time I scream for food. Usually, this is the time I demand service. But I am cautious today. I don't want to jar the silence.

I walk to my bowl. It is full of the Good Food—the expensive tuna. It has been sitting there for an hour, the edges drying out. I sniff it. My stomach wakes up. The hunger roars to life—I haven't wanted to eat in days.

I take a bite. I chew carefully. I keep the food on the left side of my mouth, away from the sore chin. *Crunch. Swallow.* It works. My jaw moves. The skin stretches, but it doesn't tear. I take another bite. Then another.

The Witch doesn't move. She watches me over the rim of her mug. She is barely breathing. She thinks if she moves, she will break the spell.

I pretend not to notice her staring. I pretend this is normal. I eat until the bowl is clean. Then I lick the ceramic.

I look up.

"Good girl," she whispers. Her voice is thick. "That's a good girl."

I turn away. I have eaten. Now I must wash.

This is the true test. I lift my paw. I hesitate. My tongue is rough; my face is raw. One wrong move and I could open everything up again.

I decide to start with the shoulder. The safe zone. *Lick. Lick.* It feels good. To be clean. To remove the smell of the hospital, the smell of the bleach, the smell of the fear. I wash my shoulder. I wash my leg.

I stop. I am tired. Eating and washing has exhausted me. The medicine makes me heavy.

I walk to the rug. Jake is there. He has been watching,

too. He is curled in a tight orange ball, one eye open. He sees me approach. He lifts his head. He doesn't run. He doesn't cringe.

I lie down next to him. Not touching. Just close. He lowers his head. He exhales.

We are not fighting. We are not hiding from each other. This is enough for now.

The day is a series of alarms.

Every few hours, the Witch's pocket watch clicks. *Click-click-click.* It is the Serum time.

Before, I would run. I would force her to hunt me.

Today, the alarm goes off at noon. I am sleeping in a sunbeam—a real, warm sunbeam that feels like a blanket instead of an oven. The Witch stands up. She goes to the pantry. I hear the glass bottle clink. I hear the ice pack being unwrapped.

She comes into the living room. She kneels down.

"Missi?" she says softly. "It's time."

I open my good eye. I look at her.

I could run. I could scramble under the sofa. I could make her drag me out. But I am warm. And my eye actually feels... dry. It feels thirsty for the drop.

I don't move.

She reaches for me. Her hands are shaking slightly. She expects the fight. I don't fight. I just tilt my chin up.

She blinks, surprised. She moves fast, not wasting the opportunity. She holds my eye open.

Drop.

The cold serum hits the lens. It washes over the ulcer. It feels amazing. Like drinking cold water on a hot day. The itch, which had been starting to creep back, is instantly drowned.

"Oh," the Witch breathes. "Okay. Good job."

She waits five minutes. I stay in the sunbeam. She gives me the antibiotic.

Drop.

"All done," she says. She strokes my back once—carefully—and then retreats.

I put my head back down on my paws.

I am learning. The Witch is not the enemy. The drops are annoying, but they are the only thing standing between me and the darkness. I can tolerate the drops.

By mid-afternoon, the house is quiet. The rain has stopped. The ledger is open on the table, and the Witch is scratching numbers out, her brow furrowed.

I know that look. That is the "Not Enough Money" look.

She sighs, rubbing her temples. She looks small.

I feel restless. My skin prickles, but not with pain. I want... something. I test the feeling. Is it hunger? No. Is it thirst? No. Is it pain? No.

I want to be touched. Not held down. Not medicated. *Touched.*

I haven't been petted—really petted—in weeks. Every touch has been medical. Every hand has held a needle, or a dropper, or a restrainer. I have been handled like a broken thing, not a cat.

I miss her hands. The old hands. The ones that knew exactly where the good spots were.

I stand up. My legs are stiff, but they hold. I walk to the table. I jump up onto the bench next to her.

She freezes. Her pen stops moving. She looks at me sideways, afraid to startle me.

I step onto the table. I walk across the ledger, blurring the ink on the "Debt" column. I stop in front of her.

I look at her hand. It is resting on the paper. It is scarred from my claws. It is stained with ink and potion.

I lower my head. I bump my forehead against her knuckles. I aim for the safe spot—the top of my skull, between the ears. If it hurts, I will know immediately.

Bump.

It doesn't hurt.

She makes a small, choked sound.

"Hi," she whispers.

I bump her again. Harder. *Pet me.*

She turns her hand over. She lifts her fingers. She is so careful. She moves like I am made of glass. Her fingers find the spot behind my right ear—the good ear.

Scritch.

Oh. My eyes close involuntarily.

Scritch. Scritch.

It feels like relief. It feels like finally drinking after a long thirst.

She moves to the neck. She digs her fingers into the thick fur of my ruff. She finds the tension knots there and works them out. I press into her hand. I push back. *Harder.*

She laughs. A wet, shaky laugh.

"You like that?" she asks.

I don't answer. I just arch my back.

She moves down my spine. She avoids the ribs (too thin). She avoids the flanks (too sensitive). She goes to the base of the tail. *The Elevator Butt spot.* She scratches.

My tail goes up. I can't help it. The machinery works.

And then, the sound starts.

It begins deep in my chest, under the ribs, under the fear. A vibration. A rattle.

Purr.

It isn't the rusty, broken purr of last week. It is a real one. It is steady. It is loud enough to vibrate the table.

The Witch drops her pen. She buries her face in her other hand. Her shoulders shake.

I ignore her tears. I am busy. I am being petted.

I stay there for ten minutes. I let her worship me. I let her remind me that I am not just a patient. I am the Queen.

When I have had enough, I step away. I shake my coat out. I look at her. *We are okay.*

She wipes her eyes. "Thank you," she whispers.

I blink at her. *You're welcome.*

Evening comes.

The sun goes down, and the house gets cold. This is usually the time of the Hunt. The time of the new poison—the one that replaced the Oil.

The Witch gets the bottle. She gets the towel. I watch her from the rug.

I don't run.

I don't want the poison. I hate the poison. The memory of the foam makes my mouth water in a bad way. But running is exhausting. And fighting her hurts us both.

I stand up. I walk to her. I sit down in front of the chair.

She looks at me, the towel in her hands. She looks confused.

"You're... volunteering?" she asks.

I am surrendering, I correct her silently. *There is a difference.*

She wraps me in the towel. She is gentle. She doesn't have to pin me because I am not thrashing.

"Ready?" she asks.

I open my mouth.

She squirts the poison in. It burns. It tastes of lemon rot and fire. I gag. I shake my head. The foam comes—it always comes—but there is less of it because I am not hyperventilating.

She wipes my mouth quickly. She has a treat ready—a piece of dried liver. She shoves it into my mouth before the taste can settle. I chew. The liver fights the lemon. The liver wins.

"Good girl," she says. "So brave."

I am not brave. I am just practical.

I walk away to groom the shame off my face.

It is night.

The cottage is quiet. The fire is banking down.

I climb into my chair. It takes a moment to get comfortable. My feet are still tender. My eye still has the plastic shield. I can still feel the heat under my skin—faint now, but there. Waiting.

I know it isn't over.

I can feel the sickness waiting. It is part of me now, woven into my blood like the magic is. It will never truly leave. There will be other flares. There will be other bad days.

But tonight, the sores are dry. Tonight, my belly is full of tuna. Tonight, I purred.

Jake jumps up onto the chair. He hesitates on the edge. *Permission to board?*

I chirp. *Permission granted.*

He curls up next to me. He rests his chin on my flank. He is heavy and warm and smells like brother.

I close my eyes.

Maybe the drops will work. Maybe the eye will heal. Maybe the Witch will figure out the numbers in her ledger.

Maybe.

I don't know what comes next. I only know what is here: the fire is warm, my brother is close, and the pain is quiet.

That is enough.

I tuck my nose under my tail. I let the warmth pull me down into sleep.

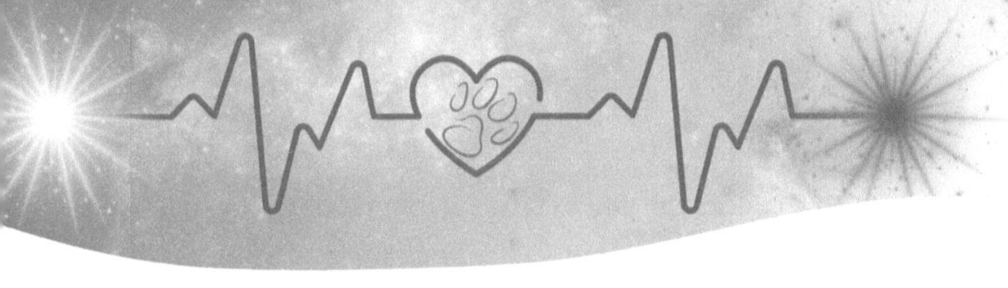

SIXTEEN

The Crash

WITCH

We go back to the Healer for the check-in.

Missi doesn't fight the carrier this time. She walks in on her own, settles into the back corner, and waits. Three weeks ago, I had to drag her out from behind the bookshelf. Now she seems to understand that the carrier means help, not betrayal. Or maybe she's just too tired to fight. I'll take either.

The Healer lifts her onto the table and shines the light. Missi squints, flattens her ears, but she doesn't scream.

"Well," the Healer says. She sounds stunned.

"What?" My stomach drops. "Is it melting again?"

"No. It's scarring."

She clicks the light off. "The ulcer has filled in. The melting has stopped. The cornea is cloudy—she will probably always have a blind spot there—but the structure is stable. The eye is saved."

I grip the edge of the metal table. The steel is cold under my fingers. *Saved.*

"And the feet?"

She checks the paws. "The swelling is down by half. The plasma cells are retreating. The pads are hardening again." She looks at me, then at the arsenal of bottles in my bag. "This is it. The combination worked. We can start stepping down."

"Stepping down?"

"The eye is healed enough that we can stop the serum drops. The antibiotic too. The ointment." She ticks them off on her fingers. "No more every-two-hours. That part is over."

I stare at her. I don't understand the words. For three weeks, my entire life has been organized around those bottles. Every two hours, day and night. The alarm. The drops. The ointment. The schedule taped to my wall, covered in check marks.

"Over?" I repeat.

"The intensive phase is done. Now we maintain. Just the suppressant, once a day. That's it."

Once a day. I think about what that means. Sleeping through the night. Not waking to alarms. Not counting the hours between doses.

"For how long?" I ask. "The suppressant?"

The Healer's expression shifts, gentler now. "Likely for the rest of her life. We might be able to lower the dose eventually, but I wouldn't plan on stopping entirely. This condition doesn't go away. It goes quiet."

I nod. I knew this. I've known this since the diagnosis. But hearing it again, after everything—it lands differently now.

"There's one more thing," the Healer says, pulling a

small sack from behind the counter. "I want to change her food. Autoimmune conditions can be triggered by proteins in the diet. The body mistakes food for invader and attacks." She opens the sack, shows me the small, uniform pellets inside. "This is hydrolyzed food. The proteins are broken down so small that her body can't recognize them as a threat."

I take the sack. It's lighter than I expected.

"It's expensive," the Healer warns. "More than regular food. But it might help prevent flares."

I look at the price tag. My stomach clenches. But I think about the cost of the Capital, the specialists, the locket I'll never get back. Prevention is cheaper than crisis. It has to be.

"I'll take it," I say.

The Healer puts her hand on my arm before I leave.

"You did a good job," she says softly. "I didn't think... honestly, when you left for the Capital, I didn't think she would come back with two eyes. You saved her."

The words land in my chest and sit there, heavy and warm. *You saved her.*

My chin starts to tremble. I dig my nails into my palm hard enough to leave crescents, fighting the pressure building behind my eyes. Not here. Not in front of the Healer. I am the one who holds it together. I am the one who makes the lists and counts the coins and gets up at two in the morning.

"Thank you," I manage.

I grab Missi. I grab the bag of expensive food. I get out the door.

I make it as far as the big oak tree on the edge of the village.

The sob comes out of nowhere—a sound that tears through my throat like something clawing its way free, and a crow startles from the branches above, wings beating hard against the leaves. I sit down hard on the bench beneath the tree, Missi's carrier pressed against my knees, and I bury my face in my hands.

I cry for the locket I sold—my mother's locket, gone forever. I cry for the fear, the nights in the Capital imagining her eye rupturing in a cage I couldn't reach. I cry for the exhaustion, three weeks of two-hour alarms, three weeks of my hands shaking so badly I could barely hold the dropper. I cry for the version of my life that existed before all this, the one where my cat was just a cat and not a patient.

Missi stirs in the carrier. She is confused by the shaking, the wet sounds. She presses her nose against the mesh, and when I open the door, she climbs into my lap and bumps her head against my chin.

I laugh. It comes out broken, half-sob. "I'm okay," I gasp, wiping my face with my sleeve. "I'm just... I'm so tired, Missi."

She settles against my chest. She doesn't understand, but she stays.

I cry until there is nothing left, until my eyes burn and my throat aches and my body feels hollow. The sun is going down. The air is cooling. Somewhere in the village, someone is cooking dinner—I can smell onions and herbs on the breeze. The ordinary scent of ordinary life, carrying on while mine fell apart.

I take a deep breath. The smell of that dinner, the feel of Missi's weight against my chest, the cooling air on my wet face—it all pulls me back into my body, into this moment, into the simple fact that I am sitting on a bench and the world is still turning.

The crisis is over.

We are not the same. We are poorer. We are scarred. We are exhausted in ways I don't have words for. But we are here.

I stop at the grocer on the way home. I buy rice, beans, and a small pot of honey because my throat is raw from crying and I want tea that doesn't taste like grief.

And I stop at the fruit crate.

Apples are expensive. They are a luxury. That copper could buy lamp oil, could patch the gap in my work boots, could go toward the debt I still owe the Eye Wizard. I should save it for the new food, the ongoing suppressant, the monthly check-ups. I pick up a red one anyway. It is heavy in my palm, and it smells like autumn, like sweetness, like something that isn't medicine.

I think about the superstition that's been living in my chest for weeks—the fear that acknowledging anything good will invite disaster back. The universe is watching, waiting for me to relax so it can strike again.

The apple sits in my hand. Four coppers of defiance.

I buy it.

I walk home with the new food in one pocket and the apple in the other, and it feels like a small act of war against the fear.

That night, I do something I haven't done in three weeks. I sleep in my own bed.

Not on the floor by the wood stove. Not on the couch with one ear listening for the alarm. My actual bed, with the quilt my grandmother made and the pillow that knows the shape of my head. When I lie down, the mattress receives me like something that's been waiting—soft where the floor was hard, warm where the stone was cold. The quilt settles over me with a weight that feels like safety instead of suffocation.

I set no alarm. There is no two-hour dose, no ointment, no serum that has to stay cold. Just the suppressant in the morning, mixed into Missi's new food.

I lie there in the dark, waiting for the panic, waiting for my body to jolt awake convinced I've forgotten something. The panic doesn't come. Instead, there is just quiet—the creak of the cottage settling, the wind in the chimney, Jake's snoring from the foot of the bed.

And then, a weight. Small, warm, settling onto the quilt near my hip.

Missi.

She hasn't slept in the bed since before the Capital. Too sore. Too wary. Too busy hiding behind the wood stove. But tonight, she is here. She circles once, twice, then curls into a tight ball against my leg. I don't move. I barely breathe.

She starts to purr.

It is a small sound—not the full-throated rattle of her healthy days, but real and steady and present. I can feel it through the bond, too, a vibration that echoes faintly in my own chest. For weeks, that connection has been nothing but static and pain. Now it hums with something quieter. Not healed. Scarred. But whole.

I close my eyes. The tears leak out sideways, soaking into the pillow.

We made it.

Morning comes slowly.

I wake to gray light and the unfamiliar sensation of being rested. Not fully—three weeks of sleep debt doesn't vanish in one night—but more rested than I've been since this all began. Missi is still on the bed. She lifts her head when I stir, blinks at me with her one clear eye and her one cloudy marble.

"Morning," I whisper.

She chirps. *Food.*

I laugh. It's a real laugh, rusty from disuse. "Yeah. Okay. Food."

I get up and go to the kitchen, measuring out the new food—the expensive hydrolyzed pellets that might help keep the fire from coming back. I mix in the suppressant, watching the powder dissolve into the kibble. One dose. Once a day. That's all.

Missi attacks the bowl like she hasn't eaten in weeks. The sound of her crunching fills the kitchen, loud and ordinary and perfect.

I make tea and eat a piece of bread, then sit at the table and look at my hands. They aren't shaking. For three weeks, they shook constantly—exhaustion, fear, too much precision work with too little sleep. I got used to gripping things harder than necessary, compensating for the tremor. Now, they are still. Steady.

I flex my fingers. Open, closed. The knuckles are dry and cracked from all the washing, all the sanitizing. But they work. They are mine again.

The days settle into a new rhythm.

Morning: suppressant in the food. Missi eats. I eat. We exist in the same space without crisis.

Afternoon: I go back to work. When I walk through the door, Bessa looks up from her ledger, takes in my hollow cheeks and the dark circles I know are still under my eyes, and nods once. "Good to have you back. You look like you've been through a war."

"Something like that," I say.

She puts me on the schedule and doesn't ask anything else. The routine of counting inventory and stocking shelves feels strange, almost foreign—normal life, after weeks of nothing but medicine and fear. But my hands remember the work even when my mind drifts, and there's comfort in the repetition.

Evening: I come home. The cottage is quiet. Missi is in her chair, or on the rug, or in the window watching birds. Jake is wherever Jake is—usually underfoot, always anxious, always checking to make sure his sister is still there. I cook dinner, do the dishes, sit by the fire and read or mend or just stare at the flames.

I keep waiting for the other shoe to drop.

The ledger tells a different story now.

I sit at the table one evening, tallying the ongoing costs. The numbers are still tight—they will always be tight—but they are different than before.

Suppressant: 15 silver per month.
Hydrolyzed food: 8 silver per month.
Monthly check-up: 3 silver.

Total: 26 silver per month.

Twenty-six silver. My wages are thirty-five. Rent is twenty. I stare at the math. It doesn't work. It has never worked.

But then I add the other column—the things I'm not buying anymore.

Serum: 0.
Antibiotic drops: 0.
Ointment: 0.
Pain medication: 0.

The crisis medications are gone. The intensive phase cost a fortune, but it's over. What remains is expensive, but it's predictable. I can plan around twenty-six silver a month. I can take extra shifts. I can skip meals when I need to.

I can survive this. As long as nothing else breaks. As long as no one gets sick, as long as the roof holds, as long as winter is mild.

I close the ledger. I don't cry. The tears are used up, for now. Instead, I just sit there, letting the numbers settle into reality.

This is our life. This is what it costs.

The following week, I do something reckless.

I go back to the apothecary. Not for medicine—I have enough for the month. I go to the basket near the register, the one with the catnip mice. The velvet-leaf ones. The expensive ones.

I pick one up. It crinkles in my hand, soft and well-made. Four coppers. I shouldn't. The math doesn't allow for luxuries. I put it back. I take a step toward the door.

I stop.

Four coppers won't save us if the fire comes back. Four coppers won't fix the roof or pay off the Wizard. But four coppers might buy ten minutes of watching my cat be a cat again, and that is worth more than lamp oil. That is worth more than being sensible.

I turn back. I pick up the mouse.

I buy it anyway.

That evening, I sit on the rug with the mouse in my hand.

"Hey, Missi."

She looks up from her chair. One ear swivels toward me.

I toss the mouse onto the rug.

She stares at it. Her whiskers twitch. For a long moment, nothing happens—she is still weak, still healing, still more interested in sleeping than playing. Then her pupils dilate. Her hindquarters shift, just slightly.

She pounces.

It's not the fluid, explosive pounce of her healthy days. It's stiff, careful, her bad eye making her misjudge the distance slightly. She lands a few inches to the left of the mouse and has to scramble to catch it. But she catches it. She grabs it in her mouth and kicks it with her back legs, rabbit-style, and a sound comes out of her—a growl, a trill, something wild and alive.

Jake's head appears from behind the sofa. His body is coiled as if ready to flee, but his tail gives a single, curious thump against the floorboards. He watches, fascinated despite himself.

Missi drops the mouse. She looks at me. Her one good eye is bright.

Again.

I toss it again. She chases it across the rug, batting it under the chair, fishing it out with one paw. I sit there on the floor, watching my broken cat play with a toy I couldn't afford, and I feel something shift in my chest. It isn't just that she's healing. It isn't just that she's playing. It's that she's still *her*—demanding, fierce, the Queen of her small domain. The sickness took her body, but it didn't take that.

Not happiness, exactly. Not yet. But something close to it. Something like hope.

Later, when the fire is burning low and the mouse has been thoroughly defeated, I sit in the armchair with my apple.

I take a bite. *Crunch.* It tastes sweet. It tastes like survival.

Missi is in her chair, curled into the "Shrimp," her nose

tucked under her tail. The fur is growing back over her scars, soft and white. Jake is asleep on the rug, his orange paw draped over the edge of the hearth, snoring softly.

They are peaceful.

This is our life now. One dose in the morning. Expensive food. Monthly check-ups. The knowledge that the fire is sleeping, not dead, and could wake at any time. But right now, in this moment, we are okay.

I finish the apple. I bank the fire. I go to bed.

Missi follows me. She curls up against my leg, purring.

I close my eyes and sleep straight through until morning.

SEVENTEEN

Good Days

MISSI

The sun is mine again.

For weeks, the sun was an enemy—too bright for my eye, too hot for my skin. I hid in the shadows behind the wood stove, a creature of dust and darkness. But today? Today, the sun is a throne.

I am in the Chair. *My* Chair. I have spent the entire morning here, moving by inches as the square of light travels across the cushion, tracking the warmth like a hunter tracks prey.

The world looks different now. My right eye sees clearly —the dust motes, the weave of the fabric, the twitch of a spider in the corner. But my left eye sees through fog. Shapes blur together. Colors smear. I have learned to turn my head more, to let the good eye do the work. It is annoying. But the fog is mine now, part of the map of me, like the scar on my tail from the cold days. I survived the burning, and the fog is the proof. I am still here to be annoyed by it.

The Witch walks into the room with her morning tea. She looks at the chair. She looks at me.

"Missi," she says. "Can I sit?"

I open one eye—the cloudy one, deliberately. It is more dismissive this way, forcing her to address a face that cannot fully see her. I give her a look that suggests she has lost her mind. *Sit? Here? In my spot?*

I stretch one leg out and spread my toes, maximizing my surface area until I am taking up ninety percent of the cushion. The sickness made me small. It made me hide. But the Chair is mine, and the hierarchy must be restored. Order begins here.

"Right," she sighs. "I guess I'll take the floor."

She sits on the rug. I close my eye. Good.

Later, the Witch tries to work.

She is at the table with the Ledger, scratching numbers, frowning, chewing on the end of her quill. I am bored. The sun has moved, and I have slept enough.

I jump onto the bench, then onto the table.

The Witch doesn't look up. "Not now, Missi. I'm trying to balance the potion budget."

Budget, shmudget.

I walk across the table and step directly onto the open book. My paw covers the "Total" column.

"Missi!"

I sit down. Right on the wet ink. I look at the quill feather bobbing in her hand. It twitches. *Toy.*

I bat at the feather.

"Stop it," she laughs, trying to push me aside. "You're smudging the ink!"

I grab the quill with both paws and bite the end of it. *Crunch.*

"Hey! That's my good pen!"

She tries to pull it away. I growl—a playful, muffled sound around the feather. I am the Pen Hunter. I have captured the prey. She lets go, and I fall back slightly, triumphant, the quill in my mouth. I drop it off the edge of the table. *Clatter.*

I look at her. *Now pick it up so we can play again.*

She shakes her head, but she is smiling. "You are a menace. A total menace."

I purr. Being a menace is hard work, but someone has to do it.

"Missi? Are you hungry?"

The voice comes from the kitchen. *Hungry?*

The endless, screaming hunger from the early medicine days is gone. But the healthy, entitled appetite of a Queen is back in full force.

I jump down from the table. My feet hit the floor with a solid *thump*—the pads healed, tough and black again. No more walking on glass. No more limping across the room like a broken thing. I walk to the kitchen and stop in the doorway.

She is preparing my bowl. The new food smells different than the old food—less like fish, more like nothing, really. The Witch says it's special, says it will help keep the burning away. I don't care what it smells like. I care that it's food.

I open my mouth. *MEOW.*

It is a demand. It is loud. It is rude. It says, *Hurry up, servant. I am wasting away.*

The Witch freezes. She looks down at me. For weeks, I have been silent, hiding behind the wood stove, too tired to complain. I do it again, putting my whole chest into it. *MOW-WOW!*

A smile breaks across her face—not the sad, watery smile of the sickroom, but a real one. And underneath it, her scent shifts. The sharp, metallic tang of fear that has clung to her for months finally begins to fade, replaced by something warmer. Something like relief.

She laughs. "Okay, Your Majesty. I'm moving as fast as I can."

She puts the bowl down. I know the medicine is in there —I can taste it sometimes, a faint bitterness under the food. But the bitterness is small. It doesn't make me foam. It doesn't make me gag. I can live with the bitterness.

I march up to the bowl and shoulder her leg out of the way. The contact is deliberate—not a request, a declaration. I remember being pinned in her lap, wrapped in towels, held down while poison filled my mouth. That was necessary, maybe, but it is over now. I am not a patient anymore. I am the Queen, and the Queen does not ask permission to eat.

I bury my face in the food. *Crunch. Smack. Swallow.*

Above me, the Witch is still laughing softly. "So bossy," she whispers. "I missed you."

I ignore her. I am eating.

Jake is a mess.

While I was sick, he let himself go. His ear is bent backward. He has a tuft of fur sticking up on his flank that looks ridiculous. But underneath the disarray, I can see the signs—a patch on his belly where the fur is too thin, licked away in anxious circles. The bald spot of a cat who has been eating his own fear. He stopped grooming himself properly. He stopped playing. He just waited, and watched, and hoped.

He is sleeping on the rug now, oblivious to his disarray.

I finish my food. I feel a burst of energy—the sudden need to run, to pounce, to be a cat again. And looking at Jake, I feel something else too. The need to fix what has gone wrong. He is my brother. He is a mess. This is unacceptable.

I run at him.

I don't limp. I gallop. My claws scramble on the wood floor—*skritch-skritch-skritch*—and I slide into him like a furry boulder. *Oof.*

Jake wakes up with a yelp. *What? Danger?*

No danger. Just sister.

I tackle his head and wrap my front paws around his neck, biting his ear—gently, just a taste. He realizes it's a game. He rolls over, kicking my stomach with his back legs, and we wrestle, a silent ball of orange and black fur rolling across the rug.

I pin him. I am smaller, but I am fiercer.

I lick his nose aggressively. *Hold still. You are dirty.*

He surrenders, going limp, and starts to purr. I groom the messy tuft on his flank. I groom his bent ear until it stands up straight. I groom his eyebrows. The fear-smell is still on him—sour, like old milk left in the sun—but it is fading now, replaced by the familiar scent of brother as I work it back into his fur.

He has been so worried. I could smell it on him all those weeks, the confusion, the desperate need to fix something he couldn't understand. He is a good brother. Even if he is afraid of brooms.

He reaches out and puts a paw over my shoulder. He pulls me in.

We collapse into a pile. I rest my chin on his orange side. He rests his chin on my back. The Witch walks by and stops. I hear the soft scratch of charcoal on paper—she is drawing us again. The sound is familiar, something from before the burning. Not the sharp scratch of the pen on the ledger, the frantic counting of coins and doses. This is softer. This is art. This is a life with room for things that aren't emergencies.

I don't move. I let her draw. We are a masterpiece.

Evening comes, and the routine is simpler now.

No more drops. No more towel. No more being held

down while stinging liquid goes into my eye. The Witch just puts the food in my bowl—the medicine already mixed in—and I eat it. That's all.

I remember the foam. I remember the taste of lemon rot and fire, the way my mouth would fill with thick white bubbles while I shook my head and tried to escape. The Witch found a different poison, a quieter one. I do not know how she did it, but she ended the Hunt. For that, I am grateful. The burning is quiet. The eye is healed—cloudy, but healed. The only reminder is the bitter taste in my food, and that is a small price.

When the meal is finished, the Witch sits in the armchair by the fire and puts the blanket over her legs. This is the signal.

I jump up.

I land on her knees and circle three times, finding the right spot, testing the give of the blanket. Then I settle down. Her hand comes down, and the touch is different now. She isn't shaking anymore. She isn't checking for heat or blood or swelling. She is just petting her cat.

And through the touch, I feel something else—the hum of the bond between us, steady and clear. For weeks, that connection was nothing but static and pain, the magic misfiring, the Unbinding tearing us apart from the inside. Now it flows quiet and warm, scarred but whole. She feels it too. I can tell by the way her breathing slows, by the way her hand gentles on my fur.

She strokes my back. She scratches the base of my ears.

I close my eyes. The purr starts.

It rattles in my chest, vibrates through my ribs, down into her legs. Deep and steady, the sound of contentment.

I am tired. The day of sun-worshipping and pen-stealing and brother-wrestling has worn me out. I will probably always be a little tired now. The sickness took something from me that I won't get back—I can feel it in my bones, a slowness in my pounce, a need for more sleep than I used to need. My body requires longer to recover from even a good day. But I am warm.

The Witch's hand rests on my side. The fire heats my face. Jake is sleeping by our feet, snoring softly.

I am scarred. I am half-blind. I will never be quite the cat I was before. But I am here. I am fed. I am warm. I am loved.

I tuck my nose under my tail. I let the darkness come, because I know now that the sun will come back in the morning.

I sleep.

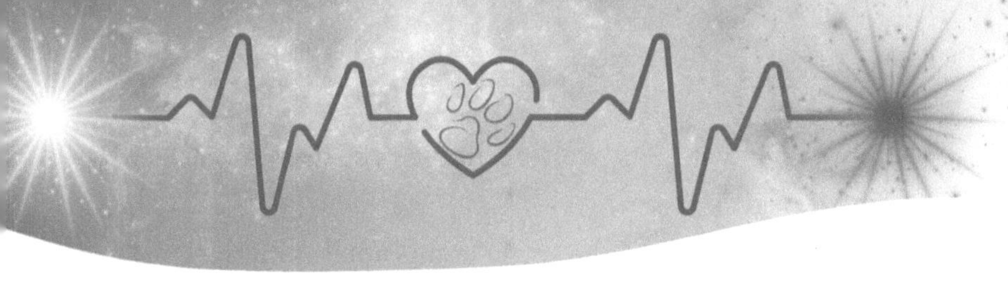

EIGHTEEN

Living With

WITCH

The morning routine is simple now.

I wake up, feed the cats, mix the powder into Missi's food—a quick stir, watching it dissolve into the expensive hydrolyzed kibble. She eats it without complaint. The bitterness is familiar now, just part of what food tastes like.

That's it. That's the whole ritual.

I remember the early days. The chart taped to the wall, covered in check marks. The two-hour alarms. The serum that had to stay cold, the sharp chemical smell of it filling my nose as I fumbled with the dropper at three in the morning. The ointment, the antibiotic, the burrito wrap and the foam and Missi's heart hammering against my palm while I held her down. The headaches that lived behind my eyes for weeks, born of exhaustion and fear.

That feels like another lifetime.

We are three months out from the Capital now. Three months of the suppressant in her food, once a day. Three months of watching, waiting, hoping the fire stays asleep. It has stayed asleep.

The Healer used the word "remission" at our last visit. She said it carefully, like she was afraid to jinx it. "The skin is quiet," she said, running her fingers over Missi's ears. "No active lesions. No inflammation. If she stays like this for another month, we can try tapering the suppressant."

Tapering. Reducing. Eventually, maybe, stopping.

I don't let myself hope too hard. I've learned that lesson. When I get home, I open the ledger and write not a "cure date" but a "reassessment date"—one month from now, with a question mark beside it. This is what planning looks like when there's no finish line. But I let myself breathe a little easier.

The panic hasn't gone away. It has just changed shape.

In the beginning, the panic was a bonfire—loud, hot, consuming everything. Now it is a candle flame. Small. Contained. But still burning. It flares at odd moments.

Mid-morning. I am washing dishes. Missi is sitting on the rug, grooming herself. She lifts her back leg. She scratches her ear. *Scritch-scritch-scritch.*

I freeze. The plate in my hand stops moving. Is she scratching because she has an itch? Or is she scratching because it's coming back?

I hold my breath. I count the scratches. *One. Two. Three.*

She stops. She licks her paw. She goes back to sleep.

I make myself exhale. I set the plate down because my hands are trembling. *Just an itch,* I tell myself. *Cats have itches. It's allowed.* But I can't let it go. I never can.

I dry my hands and walk over to her, keeping my movements casual. "Hey, buddy. Just checking."

I kneel down and inspect the ear. The skin is pink. Not red. *Pink.* The scar tissue is white and smooth. There is no heat. There is no crust.

"Okay," I whisper. "We're good."

She gives me a look of pure disdain—*why are you touching my ear, I was sleeping*—and tucks her head back under her tail.

This is my life now. The constant scanning. The vigilance that never fully turns off. I know her signs better than I know my own body. I know that if she sleeps in the tight ball—the "Shrimp"—she is fine. If she sleeps in the "Loaf," she is fine. But if she sleeps crouched, with her head low and her eyes half-open, that's pain. I know that if she eats the center of the bowl, she's happy. If she picks at the edges, her mouth hurts. I know the angle of her whiskers when she's content. I know the set of her ears when something is wrong.

We have learned a new language, she and I. Today, the language says: *Good Day.*

I kiss her head. She tolerates it. I go back to the dishes.

The flare comes in the fourth month.

I almost miss it. It's evening, and I'm sitting by the fire, mending a hole in my work apron, when Missi jumps onto the arm of the chair. She does this sometimes—demands proximity without demanding touch. I've learned to appreciate the distinction.

She settles. I keep sewing.

Then she shakes her head. A quick, sharp motion.

I look up. She does it again. Shake. Then her back paw comes up, and she scratches behind her left ear.

My needle stops moving.

It's nothing, I tell myself. *Cats scratch.*

But I'm already setting the mending aside. I'm already reaching for her, slowly, giving her time to pull away. "Let me see, sweetheart."

She lets me turn her head. She's learned that resistance just prolongs the inspection.

I look at the ear. At first, I don't see anything. The skin is pink, the fur is growing in thick and soft, the scars are—

There.

A small spot, just inside the ear canal. Pinker than the surrounding skin. Slightly raised.

A phantom smell fills my nose—bleach and ozone, the sterile chill of the Capital's waiting room. My hands go cold, the memory of the dropper slick between my fingers.

"Okay," I say. My voice is steady. I am proud of that. "Okay. We caught it."

We go back to the Healer the next morning.

She examines the spot, takes a scraping, looks at me with an expression I can't quite read.

"It's a small flare," she says. "Very small. You caught it early."

"What do we do?"

"We go back up on the suppressant. Full dose, for two weeks. Then we reassess."

Two weeks. Not two months. Not a trip to the Capital. Not a melting eye and swollen paws and a cat who hides behind the wood stove. Just two weeks.

"The fact that you caught it this early is good," the Healer says, writing out the prescription, her quill scratching against the paper. "This is what management looks like."

I nod. I take the prescription.

I don't cry until I'm outside, leaning against the wall of the Healer's cottage, letting the tears come fast and silent. My legs feel weak beneath me, and a knot I didn't know was there finally unclenches in my stomach. It's a breath I've been holding for months escaping all at once.

They're not sad tears. Not entirely. They're relief tears. We caught it. We knew what to look for. The months of vigilance paid off.

And standing there, wiping my face on my sleeve, I finally understand what winning looks like now. It's not a cure. It's not an ending. It's small flares, caught fast, treated quickly. It's not failure. It's the system working.

Two weeks later, the spot is gone.

The Healer examines Missi again, running her fingers over the ear, checking the chin, the nose, the paws. "Back to maintenance dose," she says. "And we watch."

We always watch. That part never changes. But the crisis was small. The recovery was fast. And I handled it without falling apart.

That feels like progress.

I go to the Apothecary on Thursday.

The bell chimes when I walk in. The old man behind the counter looks up, and his face creases into a smile. "Afternoon. The usual?"

"Just the suppressant. And a bag of the liver treats."

He reaches under the counter and pulls out the familiar bottle. The glass is dark, the label worn from handling. I've bought so many of these.

"How's she doing?"

"Stable," I say. "We had a small flare last month, but we caught it early."

"That's the way," he nods. "Catch it early, treat it fast. You've got good eyes."

I pay him. The coins leave my purse easily now.

I used to resent the money. I used to count every copper and think about the things I couldn't buy, the repairs I couldn't make, the life I couldn't live. I don't think about that anymore. This is just what it costs to have Missi. Like firewood. Like food. Like rent. A line item in the ledger of my life.

My magic has always been about maintenance—patching the roof, keeping out drafts, binding the fraying edges of things that won't stay whole on their own. This cost is just another form of that same mundane, essential work. Not glamorous. Not powerful. Just necessary.

The numbers are tight. They will always be tight. But they balance—as long as I eat rice and foraged greens most nights, as long as the extra shifts at Bessa's keep coming, as long as nothing else breaks.

I walk home with the bottle in my pocket, warm from my hand.

Six months out from the Capital.

The Healer uses a new word: "stable remission."

"We can try reducing the dose," she says. "Half strength for a month. If she stays clear, we can try every other day. Eventually, we might be able to stop entirely—just watch and treat flares as they come."

I stare at her. "Stop entirely?"

"Some cats can go months, even years, between flares

once they're stable. It's not a cure—the condition is still there, sleeping. But it's possible to manage it without daily medication."

I think about what that would mean. No more powder in her food. No more monthly refills at the apothecary. Just watching. Waiting. Trusting that I'll catch it if it comes back. Terrifying, because what if I miss a spot on her ear and we end up back in the Capital? Freedom, because I could finally afford to fix the roof before winter.

"Let's try it," I say.

The taper is slow.

Half dose for a month. She stays clear. Every other day for a month. She stays clear. Every third day. Clear.

Then, one morning, I measure out the powder. My hand hovers over the bowl, the familiar motion of stirring it in ready to begin. I stand there for a long moment, looking at the white powder in the measuring spoon, looking at the bowl of food, looking at Missi sitting on the counter watching me with impatient eyes.

I put the spoon down. I tip the powder back into the jar.

I watch her eat. I watch her groom. I watch her chase Jake across the living room and knock over the stack of books by the window.

She's fine. The next day, she's still fine. The day after that, she's still fine.

I keep watching. I will always keep watching. But the

bottles are in the cabinet now, not on the counter. The chart is off the wall. The faint chemical smell of medicine and bleach that lingered in the cottage for months has finally faded, replaced by woodsmoke and the herbs drying in the window. The routine has simplified to its essence: look, assess, trust.

Evening falls.

This is my favorite time. The work is done, the fire is lit, the cottage smells like home again. I sit in the armchair with the ledger open on my lap and a bowl of rice and foraged greens cooling on the side table—dinner, same as most nights now. The sacrifice that makes the numbers work.

The numbers look different now. The medication line is smaller—just the emergency supply I keep on hand, just in case. The food is still expensive, but I've found a rhythm. Extra shifts when I need them. Simpler meals for myself. Small luxuries, carefully chosen.

I bought myself new boots last month. The old ones had holes. I'd been putting it off for over a year, choosing the boots over finally replacing my thin cloak. There's always a trade. But my feet are dry now, and winter is still months away.

Rent: Paid. Food: Paid. Emergency fund: 8 silver.

Eight silver. It's not much. But it exists. A cushion between us and disaster.

I close the ledger and look up.

Missi is in her chair, washing Jake, her tongue rasping rhythmically over his ear. He is lying on his back, belly exposed, purring so loudly I can hear it from across the room. A log shifts in the fire with a sudden crack, and Jake flinches—but he doesn't run. His head turns immediately toward Missi, checking that she's safe, before he settles back down. That's new. My anxious orange boy, who used to hide under the bed at every loud noise, now holds his ground when his sister needs him.

She pauses. She looks at me.

Her good eye is bright green. Her bad eye is a cloudy pearl—she'll never see clearly out of it, but she's learned to compensate. Her ears are scarred but furred. Her chin is smooth. She looks like a survivor. Because that's what she is.

She chirps. *What? Why are you staring?*

"Nothing," I whisper. "Just looking."

She holds my gaze for a moment. Then she goes back to grooming Jake, dismissing me entirely.

I smile.

I am tired.

Not the bone-deep exhaustion of the crisis months—that has faded, mostly. But a quieter tired. The tired of someone who has been through something and come out the other side.

I will always be a little tired now. I will always be watching for the signs—and through the bond, I feel an echo of that vigilance, a phantom itch along the connection between us whenever my anxiety spikes. I've learned to shield her from my own stress, to breathe through the fear instead of letting it flow down the line. Even my worry could trigger a flare. So I watch, and I breathe, and I keep my fear contained.

That's the price of loving something fragile.

But look at them.

Missi, queen of her chair, grooming her brother with the casual authority of royalty. Jake, trusting and soft, letting her fix the fur he can't reach himself. The fire crackling. The wind quiet outside.

We made it.

I pick up the mending I set aside earlier—the hole in my work apron, half-stitched. The needle moves through the fabric, pulling the torn edges together. Not making it new. Just making it strong enough to keep working. That's what I did for Missi, isn't it? That's what I did for us. Not a cure. Not a return to before. Just careful stitches, holding the pieces together, making something that can last.

Not to a finish line—there is no finish line. Not to a cure—there is no cure. But to something sustainable. Something that looks like life.

I lean back in the chair. I close my eyes.

Tomorrow I will wake up and check her ears. I will watch her eat and note how she moves and catalog every scratch and shake. I will carry the weight of knowing what could happen, what has happened, what might happen again.

But tonight, the fire is warm. The cats are peaceful. The house is standing.

Life goes on.

That's the whole miracle, isn't it? After the endless nights where sleep was a currency measured in two-hour increments, after the metallic taste of fear in the Capital, life just... goes on.

Missi jumps down from her chair. She crosses the room and pauses at my feet, looking back at her own chair, then up at me. I watch her weigh the options—the familiar throne, or the offered lap. After a long moment, she jumps up and settles against my chest.

She doesn't do this often anymore. She's more independent now, more careful about who she lets close. But tonight, she chooses me.

I rest my hand on her back. I feel her breathing, slow and even. I feel the vibration of her purr starting up, rusty at first, then smoothing out into a steady rumble.

"Good girl," I whisper. "My good, brave girl."

She doesn't answer. She's already asleep.

I stay very still, letting her rest, letting the fire burn down, letting the night settle around us.

This is what living with looks like.

It's not the life I imagined. It's harder, and more expensive, and more frightening than I ever thought it would be.

But it's ours.

And that's enough.

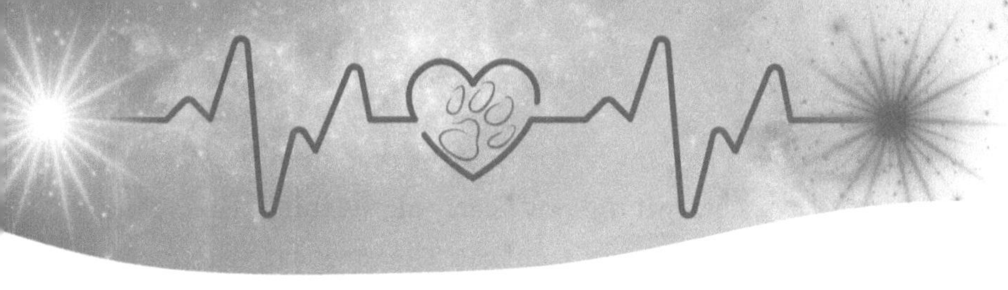

NINETEEN

Home

MISSI

The sun finds me first.

It always does. I have trained it well.

I am in the Chair—my Chair—watching the light crawl across the floorboards. It moves slowly, but I am patient. I have nowhere else to be. The cottage is quiet. The Witch is still asleep. Jake is an orange lump on the rug, his paws twitching as he chases dream-mice. The fire has burned down to embers, but the room holds the warmth like a memory.

I stretch. Back legs first, pushing against the armrest until my claws catch the weave. Then the front. Spine arching. A long pull of muscle and fur.

I pause, waiting for the protest—the ache in my joints, the pull of tight skin. It doesn't come. Everything moves the way it should.

This still surprises me, some mornings. I remember when stretching meant pain. When moving meant fire. When my own skin was the enemy. That time is part of me now, woven into my history like the scar on my tail from the cold days. I carry it the way I carry all the things that made me who I am. Not a different cat. The same cat, with more maps drawn on her body.

My world is different than it used to be.

It looks different. My left eye—the one that melted and came back—sees the room through a permanent fog. The Witch is a blurry shape on that side. The furniture has soft edges. When Jake approaches from the left, I don't see him until he's close enough to smell. I have learned to turn my head more. I listen harder. I rely on my whiskers to tell me where the walls are, where the table ends, where the drop begins.

It is annoying. But it is mine.

My body feels different, too. The burning is gone, but it left marks. My skin feels tighter than it used to, especially around my ears. The scars itch when it rains—a dull, distant itch, nothing like the screaming fire of before, but there. A reminder.

I move slower now. Before the sickness, I would fly across the room. I would leap from the floor to the top of the cabinet in a single bound, landing light as dust. Now, I test things first. I look at a jump and I think: *Can I make that? Is the landing soft enough?* Usually, I take the chair instead. I take the stairs. I find the easier path.

Some might call this weakness. I call it wisdom. I save

my energy for the things that matter. The sunbeam. The dinner cry. The purr.

The Witch wakes up.

I hear her stirring in the bedroom—the creak of the bed, the shuffle of feet on cold floorboards. She appears in the doorway, hair tangled, eyes still soft with sleep. She sees me in the Chair. She smiles.

"Morning, Missi."

I blink at her. *Morning. You're late. The sun has been up for hours.*

She meets my gaze and holds it for a moment—then gives me a slow, deliberate blink. I know this gesture. It means trust. It means *I see you and I am not afraid.* She holds the blink for a heartbeat, then turns to walk to the kitchen to make her tea.

This is new. This took a long time.

For months, she watched me constantly. Every scratch, every shake of my head, every time I rubbed my face against the furniture—her eyes would snap to me, her body would tense, and I would feel her fear like a cold wind through the bond between us.

She still watches. I know she does. But it's quieter now. She trusts that I am okay. She trusts that if I'm not okay, she will see it in time. Our trust was rebuilt day by day. She watched, and I healed. It was enough.

The burning sleeps. It might wake up—I know this, the

way I know the weather will change and the mice will hide in winter. It is part of me now, a quiet hum along the bond between us, not painful anymore but always present. The Unbinding left its mark on the magic that connects us, a scar in the current that will never fully smooth.

But it has been sleeping for a long time. And I am tired of waiting for it.

I live now. That is enough.

I leap down from the Chair and head for the kitchen without waiting for her. I have places to be.

Breakfast is simple.

The Witch puts food in my bowl. The new food—the one that smells like nothing and tastes like nothing but doesn't make the burning angry. I have learned to eat it without complaint. It fills my belly. It keeps me safe.

No medicine today. No bitter powder mixed into the kibble. The bottles are in the cabinet now. I can smell them sometimes—that sharp, chemical tang—when the Witch opens the door. The smell still makes something in me flinch, a ghost of the foam and the fight. But underneath the fear-memory, there is something else: the knowledge, deep in my bones, that those smells are connected to the pain going away. The bottles hurt me. The bottles saved me. Both things are true.

They stay in the cabinet. They are for emergencies. For if the burning wakes up.

It hasn't woken up.

I eat my breakfast, clean my whiskers, and walk to the window to watch the birds.

Jake finds me on the windowsill.

He jumps up beside me—clumsy, too big for the narrow ledge, his orange bulk crowding me toward the glass.

Move over, I tell him with a flick of my ear.

He doesn't move over. He never does. He just settles his weight against my side and starts to purr.

He is ridiculous. He is afraid of brooms. He is afraid of loud noises and sudden movements and his own shadow when the light hits it wrong. But he was not afraid to sit by the wood stove when I was a monster spitting fire. He was not afraid to scratch at the door when I hissed at everyone who came near. When the whole world was too much to bear, he waited.

He is not afraid of me.

He was, for a while. During the worst of it, when I hissed at him and swiped at his face and hid in corners where he couldn't follow. He didn't understand why I had changed. He just knew that his sister was gone and something angry had taken her place. But he waited. He kept coming back. He would sit outside whatever door I was behind and scratch, scratch, scratch until I let him in.

He is a good brother.

I lean into his warmth. I let him groom my bad ear—

the one with the scars, the one that's sensitive to touch. He is the only one allowed. His tongue rasps over the tight, slick scar tissue where the fur won't grow back, then moves to the softer patch where the new fur came in white and downy. He knows exactly how much pressure I can stand, knows where the map of my healing has drawn its borders.

We sit in the window together, watching the birds, breathing in time.

The afternoon is for sleeping.

I return to my Chair. The sun has moved to the perfect spot—a warm square on the cushion, waiting for me. I circle once, twice. I knead the fabric, feeling it give under my paws. I lie down.

The warmth soaks into my fur, into my skin, into my bones. I feel my eyes getting heavy. The sounds of the cottage fade—the scratch of the Witch's pen, the crackle of the fire, Jake's snoring from the rug. I drift.

I dream of running. In the dream, my legs are strong and I am chasing something through tall grass—a mouse, a leaf, a shadow. The world is blurry on one side, shapes smearing together at the edge of my vision, but I have learned to turn my head. I track the prey with my good eye. I compensate. I adapt. I don't catch it. I don't need to catch it. The chase is the point.

I wake up to the Witch's hand on my back.

"Hey, sleepy girl," she says softly. "You've been out for hours."

I stretch and yawn, showing all my teeth. *I was busy. Important cat business.*

She scratches behind my good ear. I let her.

Evening comes.

The light turns gold, then orange, then fades to gray. The Witch lights the fire. The cottage fills with the smell of woodsmoke and the herbs drying in the window. This is my favorite time.

I jump onto the Witch's lap. She makes room for me, shifting the book she was reading, adjusting the blanket over her legs. I circle. I knead. I settle. Her hand finds the spot at the base of my tail. She scratches.

The purr starts.

It is deep and steady, rattling through my chest, vibrating against her legs. It is the sound of contentment. The sound of home.

I close my eyes.

I think about the sickness, sometimes. The fire that ate my face. The fog that swallowed my eye. The days I spent hiding behind the wood stove, too tired to move, too hurt to be touched. I think about the Witch holding me down. The drops. The foam. The taste of medicine and the smell of fear. I think about how close I came to losing this—the Chair, the sunbeam, the lap, the purr.

The fire took its portion. But this remained.

The burning might come back. The Witch will watch for it. She will catch it early, like she did before. She will put the bitter powder back in my food, and I will eat it, and we will fight the fire together. Or the burning might stay asleep forever. I might live out my days in this cottage, in this chair, in this square of sun, and never feel the fire again.

I don't know which one will happen. I can't know.

But I am a cat. The past is a bad smell. The future is a sound I can't hear. But the fire is warm on my face. The Witch's hand is on my back. This is real.

And in the now, the cushion is soft. My belly is full. The fire is warm. My brother is sleeping on the rug. The Witch's hand is gentle on my back.

My fur is thinner over the scars. My world is foggy on one side. These are the marks of the journey. They are the map that proves I found my way back.

But I am here.

I am home.

I tuck my nose under my tail. I let the warmth pull me down into sleep, and I do not dream of fire.

I dream of sun.

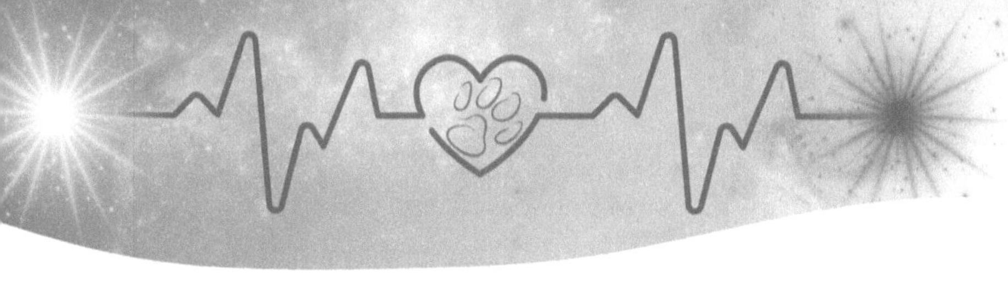

Afterword

Author's Note

The story is fiction, but the heart of it is entirely real.

Missi is based on my own cat, Ripley, who was diagnosed with Pemphigus Foliaceous, a rare autoimmune skin condition. Like the Witch in the story, I found myself thrust into a world of specialists, confusing medical terms, and a rollercoaster of hope and heartbreak.

When Ripley was diagnosed, I felt incredibly alone. Pemphigus is not a common ailment; you can't just ask your neighbor about it. The journey of a caregiver for a chronically ill pet is a silent one. It is waking up at dawn to give meds. It is the constant scanning for new scabs. It is the financial panic. And it is the crushing weight of making medical decisions for a creature who cannot understand why you are doing this to them.

I wrote this story to process that journey. I wrote it for the caregivers—the ones who are tired, the ones who are broke, and the ones who are currently sitting on the floor with a towel and a syringe, crying because they have to be the "bad guy" to save their best friend.

You are not alone. And as long as they are purring, there is hope.

— Kysa Steele

Signs to Watch For

If you notice any of the following symptoms in your cat, please consult a veterinarian or a veterinary dermatologist. Early detection can make a massive difference in treatment outcomes.

- **Crusty lesions or scabs:** Usually starting on the bridge of the nose, the tips of the ears, and around the nail beds.
- **Pustules:** Small, pimple-like bumps on the skin.
- **Violent itching:** Scratching the face or ears to the point of bleeding.
- **"Pillow Foot":** Paw pads that look swollen, mushy, or have a purple hue.
- **Thickened or crusty discharge** around the nail beds (Paronychia).
- **Lethargy and fever:** In severe cases, the cat may seem depressed or stop eating.

A Note on Ripley

Ripley is still with us.

She is the Queen of the house, the ruler of her domain, and a professional menace to her siblings. She is not "cured" —she will likely be on medication for the rest of her life— but she is happy.

She has her spot in the sun. She has her appetite. And on the good days, she has her cattitude.

To anyone currently in the thick of the "Morning War" with the meds: **Keep going.** It gets easier. The routine becomes rhythm, the panic becomes management, and the purrs... the purrs are worth every single struggle.

🤍 Kysa & Ripley

About the Author

Kysa Steele is an IT professional by day, and by night an author, TTRPG GM, cat servant, and wife (though the order depends on which cat is asking). She grew up devouring books and plotting to write her own. While newly minted as an indie author, she's been telling elaborate, occasionally cursed stories at the TTRPG table for years.

Her cat-centric fiction spans dark fantasy, detective noir, portal adventures, and apocalyptic comedy. The Infurnal Catastrophe series features a cursed demon princess and infernal magic, while the Orange Protocol follows a hard-boiled detective trapped in a cat's body and scattered across a psychic network of orange tabbies. Her Unfamiliar Territory series stars Mischief, a portal-hopping cat whose curiosity threatens entire dimensions. She spends her time building worlds and trying to unravel her cats' many conspiracies.

She lives in Texas with her husband and a cadre of furry overlords. Nori and Mochi are the latest recruits, while Nox, nicknamed the Demon Princess, claimed dominion during the writing of Curse Meow Not. Jake Speed and his sister Ripley occupy the middle ranks, and the eldest, Cid, remains her watchful shadow and self-appointed bodyguard.

Cat Out of Luck

Mischief just wanted to jazz up a boring ritual, nap, and maybe snag a few sardines for later. Instead, he got trapped in a human body and discovered something is hunting familiars across dimensions, harvesting them as magical batteries. The universe made a terrible mistake giving him any responsibility. He's going to make it everyone's problem.

The Twelve Days of Catmas

Krampus has spent three hundred years alone in his lair, filing suffering reports and telling himself he's fine. Then a small black cat shows up and refuses to leave. Each day brings new chaos— argumentative partridges, therapy doves, unionizing hens, explosive geese. What Krampus doesn't know is that Yule isn't just a cat. He's the Spirit of Festive Misrule, and every disaster is surgical precision designed to crack through centuries of isolation. Therapy has never been this catastrophic. Or this purr-suasive.

Nine Lives, Zero Paperwork

Brentley didn't mean to become a cosmic fugitive. He just wanted a ride. But when an orange tabby with reality-warping powers and a pathological lying problem hijacks cargo hauler Jarik Venn's ship, things spiral fast. The Familiar Reclamation Bureau—a hyper-bureaucratic agency staffed by disgruntled former familiars—wants Brentley back. Brentley wants to be worshipped as the god-king he clearly is. Jarik just wants his ship to stop being on fire. Between hairballs that violate physics and a cat who takes credit for every accident, this might be the worst day of Jarik's life. Or the start of something he'll never escape.

The Cat Who Ate the End of the World

Mungus ate the apocalypse. It tasted like chicken. Now he's a cosmically significant cat with reality-warping indigestion, Claire is fighting a government committee that wants to "contain" him, and a paperwork-loving demon named Harold has discovered that bureaucracy is actually a form of love. The fish showers are getting worse. The traffic lights are speaking Sumerian. And somewhere in London, a very important cat just wants to go home to his person —even if it means trusting her through the scariest thing of all: asking for help.

Want more cats and chaos?

Join my Patreon for weekly chapter drops, exclusive stories, world-building lore, and behind-the-scenes chaos at patreon.com/kysasteele

Enjoyed this book?

Reviews help other readers find these stories! If you have a moment, leaving a review on Amazon, Goodreads, or your retailer of choice means the world to indie authors like me.

Want a free short story?

Sign up for my newsletter and get 2 short stories from my other series. **kysasteele.com/newsletter**

www.ingramcontent.com/pod-product-compliance
Lightning Source LLC
Chambersburg PA
CBHW020111310726
48970CB00002B/574